SPUR
AND
THE GUNFIGHTER

Spur held his breath, refined the sight again on the shoulder, and squeezed off the shot.

The blast of the .44 round came like a thunderclap, only to be topped by the shouts of surprise and amazement as John Ringo took the round in his left shoulder and sprawled backwards in the dust of the unpaved street.

He glared at Spur, but his right arm hung useless. His own six-gun had spilled from leather and lay three feet away. Ringo grabbed at it with his left hand, but already Spur had sighted in and fired. The chunk of .44 caliber lead hit the cylinder of the Colt .44 and slammed it a dozen feet backwards out of the reach of John Ringo.

Spur walked up and looked down at the famous gunfighter.

"Told you I had no cause to kill you, Ringo. You go see Doc George, and then you still have forty-five minutes to be on the stage."

Odyssey
Book
Shop

565 Main St.
Lebanon
Oregon 97355
(541) 258-5353

D0047588

Also in the SPUR Series:

SPUR #17

SALOON GIRL

Dirk Fletcher

LEISURE BOOKS ∞ NEW YORK CITY

A LEISURE BOOK

Published by

Dorchester Publishing Co., Inc.
6 East 39th Street
New York, NY 10016

Copyright©1986 by Chet Cunningham

All rights reserved. No part of this book may be reproduced or transmitted in any form or by any electronic or mechanical means, including photocopying, recording, or by any information storage and retrieval system, without the written permission of the Publisher, except where permitted by law.

Printed in the United States of America

Saloon Girl

1

There was a starkly beautiful place where the trail topped the last hill and fell away from the blue sky with its fleeting white clouds and raced downward toward the green of the valley floor along the river, then stretched farther east and north into town. This was a place a man could look down on the world spread out before him, watch the hawks circling far below in their graceful, constant search. Along this trail a man came riding.

John Ringo pulled up his bay mare where the trail slanted down and sat a moment staring out at the quiet valley of the Grande Ronde river. He never thought he would get to Oregon, and never this far off the well traveled routes.

He had been visiting his three sisters in San Jose, halfway up the long state of California, when a letter from Texas told him an old partner of his had holed up in La Grande, Oregon, a small town out on the high and dry eastern half of the state where they raised cattle and cut timber.

It was 1867 and John Ringo never liked to let a
debt go unpaid, especially one of five hundred
dollars that was three years overdue. He cut
short his visit to his sisters, who knew him as
John Ringgold. He had changed his name so they
never would learn of his lawlessness and
reputation as an outlaw in Texas, Arizona and
half the western states. Now all he wanted was to
ride down into La Grande, find Curley Johnson
and extract the five hundred dollars.

Ringo was a tall man, almost six feet, two
inches, and Texas-lean with a somber face and
light blue eyes. He gambled, usually drank to
excess and had most of his killing fights when he
was drunk. In Tombstone, Arizona, where he
spent most of his time, he was known as the
fastest, deadliest shot around. Nobody came to
town to try to make a name for himself by
shooting it out with John Ringo.

He had taken the train up the coast and then
the stage two hundred and sixty-four miles from
Portland to La Grande. It was a rough two and a
half days in a Concord stagecoach, and Ringo felt
all tied up from the close quarters. They arrived
just after noon and he promptly rented a horse
and took a ride around the town, then up the
stage road west. Now he felt better. He would
find Curley Johnson tonight.

Ringo tipped a pint bottle of whiskey, took a
long pull and capped it.

He turned and rode down the hill into La
Grande.

By the time he tied his rented horse up in front
of the Sagebrush bar, it was dark. He went to a
small cafe nearby that offered a "one pound
steak" dinner. The steak was fair, but not Texas

quality. He told the owner so as he paid, then he turned toward the Sagebrush bar where Curley Johnson was supposed to be tonight.

His partnership with Curley was not the legal kind—quite the opposite. They had teamed up to relieve some stage coach passengers of their valuables and found a drummer traveling with over a thousand dollars in cash on him. They took it from him and left the area quickly. Much later that night after John Ringo drank himself into a stupor, Curley had relieved John of his half of the cash.

Now Ringo was going to get it back.

There was a swagger to the way John Ringo walked, and even he was not sure if he did it on purpose or if it had grown into his normal movement as a kind of warning and defensive mechanism. At any rate, it worked. His two pearl handled revolvers hung low, lean and mean and ready, and while few knew his name in Oregon, they recognized the low tied six-guns and the no-nonsense expression on his face.

Gunfighter!

Any sane man took two steps back around such a man.

He pushed his way into the Sagebrush saloon and looked around. At least it had a plank floor. There was a long bar against one side, a dozen small tables for drinking and poker, and two larger poker tables at the back. The far side held a small stage and an upright piano much the worse for wear. The music box had taken a bath in two rivers on its way across the plains twenty years ago in a covered wagon. It had been reworked and refitted but it played almost as good as new.

Ringo did not see his ex-partner at any of the

tables or at the bar. He let his right hand relax a little and strode to the bar.

"Whiskey, the good stuff, a bottle!" Ringo spat out. He took the offered bottle and glass, dropped a quarter eagle, a two and a half dollar gold piece, on the counter, and walked away. He kicked a chair back from a small table near the wall and sat down. He could see anyone who came in the door and everyone inside the gin mill.

For an hour he worked on the bottle of whiskey. It was fair, as rotgut whiskey went this far from home. Texas would always be home. But he could never go back. He had been only fifteen when a cattleman-sheep herder feud flared into violence. John's only brother was killed and he swore vengeance. He hunted down the three men responsible for his brother's murder and killed each one. Then he had to flee the state and dodge an occasional bounty hunter who came looking for him.

Now he peered over the glass and watched every man who came in the front door. There were three tainted, painted and shopworn saloon girls in the Sagebrush. Each had tried to interest him in her charms, but he had roughly pushed them all away.

By nine o'clock the fifth of whiskey was half gone. Ringo's eye was clear and he could still walk a straight line across the floor. He looked up and saw Curley Johnson walk in. He was immediately hugged by one of the bar girls who put her arm around him and headed for the back cribs. Curley pushed her away and went to the bar.

Ringo roared in anger and stood, tipping over

his small table, and smashing the whiskey bottle as it hit the floor.

"Sonofabitch!" Ringo screeched. "Curley, you thieving bastard, I'm calling you out, right now!"

Johnson turned slowly, his hands on his shoulders. He had one six-gun on his right side, tied low.

"Ringo! Wondered what happened to you when we got separated. This gang jumped me, robbed us both and . . ."

"Liar!" Ringo thundered. "You robbed *me*. I want the money back now, or a chunk of your hide!"

"Now, Ringo, take it easy. I'll make up what they stole, damned if I won't. What was it, about five hundred? I can make that up . . . sooner or later."

"*Now*, you thieving sonofabitch!"

Curley began to sweat. "Ringo, can I reach for my wallet?"

"Long as it's got money in it."

Curley brought it out. He opened it so Ringo could see the bills inside; greenbacks, several. When Ringo squinted his eyes to see the denominations, Curley dropped the wallet and his right hand darted for his hip.

It didn't look like Ringo moved quickly, but before the eye caught the jolting movement of his right hand, it came up with iron and three shots blasted by the time Curley's fingers closed around the walnut handle of his .44. He never got it out of leather.

The three rounds came fast from the double action revolver, and all three .44 caliber slugs slammed into Curley, nailing him to the bar for a moment. Two slashed through his heart, killing him instantly. The next hit his throat as his lifeless body began to fall.

The Sagebrush Saloon had gone deathly quiet as the two men argued. Prudent men edged away from the combatants, leaving an empty alley behind and between both men. The barkeep had slid well out of range and reached for a sawed-off shotgun he kept below the counter loaded with double-ought buck. He didn't need it.

By the time the apron lifted up from behind the bar, Curley was dead and John Ringo had straightened up his table, sat down and signalled one of the saloon girls to bring him more whiskey.

Five minutes later, Sheriff Quincy Younger, who was fifty-two years old and had been elected to his four year term the last four elections, walked in the door. He had the look of a lawman who would rather argue the law than try to enforce it.

Sheriff Younger was half a head shorter than Ringo and had developed a fondness for his second wife's cooking. She had twice had to let his pants out. He checked the dead man.

"Get him out the back way and over to Zed's undertaking parlor," the sheriff told two men standing nearby. They picked the body up by hands and feet and carried him through the back door.

Sheriff Younger grunted as he got off his knees after examining the corpse. He walked over to John Ringo's table and sat down.

"Evening, Sheriff. Buy you a drink?" Ringo waved to one of the girls who brought another glass. He poured two fingers of whiskey for the lawman.

Sheriff Younger took the whiskey in two gulps. He needed it. It had been six months since he'd had a killing in town. He had recognized the man in front of him at once. John Ringo was wanted in half a dozen western states and territories. Right now Sheriff Younger had no thoughts of arresting the gunsharp. Younger cleared his throat.

"Mr. Ringo, can you tell me what happened here?"

"He shot down Curley, that's what he did!" a saloon girl named Belle screeched and ran at Ringo. He held out one arm, fending her off as she swore at him and flailed her thin arms. Two men pulled her away and she calmed down.

"Sheriff, it was self defense. That man drew first. Ask anybody. He went for his six-gun, so I had to defend myself."

"Three shots?"

Ringo laughed without humor. "Five years ago, Sheriff, I might have trusted one shot. These days I'm not taking so many chances. I've seen more than one man shot down and killed after he thought he'd killed his opponent."

The sheriff looked around the saloon. He pointed at two men and motioned. They walked over.

"You both saw the killing?"

They nodded.

"Tell me what happened." He indicated one of the men.

"This man, Mr. Ringo, was in the place drinking. He had a bottle. Been here long as I have, an hour. Next thing I know, I hear him yell at the other guy, Curley. They were talking about some money, then the dead man went for his gun. He made his move first. He was just too slow."

The second man told the same story.

Sheriff Younger sighed and stood up. "Mr. Ringo. I'll go along with self defense, but I want you to come around the office tomorrow and sign a statement to that effect. All right?"

"Whatever you say, Sheriff. I was just having a few drinks."

"Will you be in town long, Mr. Ringo?"

"Not sure, I have some more business here."

"I hope nobody else owes you money."

Ringo laughed. He had frowned slightly at first, then he laughed. He had won, he was free. John Ringo felt good. One debt had been paid, with blood.

Sheriff Younger motioned to the glass. "Thanks for the drink. Now I better get back to the office."

A few minutes later, Sheriff Younger leafed through a stack of wanted posters that he had accumulated from the mail. He had heard about John Ringo for years. His usual haunts lately had been around Tombstone, Arizona where he played cat and mouse with the Earp brothers. Had Ringo come all this way just to shoot down a man who owed him money?

He found a poster. The picture was not a good likeness. The poster was from Texas where a much younger John Ringo, also known as John Ringgold, was wanted for three murders. There was a three thousand dollar reward.

The sheriff kept looking. Deeper down in the pile he found another wanted poster from New Mexico Territory. Ringo was wanted there for murder as well. Five hundred dollars reward.

Sheriff Younger pushed the posters back in the stack and stuffed them in his bottom drawer.

There was no chance that he was going to try to arrest Ringo on the strength of the posters. Texas was too far away. He couldn't spare a deputy to take Ringo back. If any of them lived through trying to arrest Ringo. No, there was not the ghost of a hope that he would arrest John Ringo.

When someone opened the front door, he looked up to see his wife coming in with a late night snack in a small basket. She brought it every night he worked.

Charlotte Younger was twenty-six, half his age. She had been a widow for a year when he married her. He couldn't ask for a better wife. She was so young and fresh and beautiful that he said a prayer of thanks every day. She had flowing black hair she kept long at his insistence. It framed her face and swept half way down her back.

"Pumpkin pie with whipped cream!" Charlotte said, uncovering the dish containing the quarter of a pie wedge.

She sobered. "I hear there was some trouble."

"All taken care of. Self defense. No problem."

Charlotte smiled and pushed a strand of greying hair back behind his ear. "Good, because even I have heard of John Ringo. He's a bad one. I hope he leaves town soon." She took a big breath and hugged him.

"Quincy, I had one husband killed while he worked out of this office. I am certainly not going to allow that to happen a second time!"

Sheriff Younger chuckled and kissed her soft cheek. "Sweet Charlotte, I am on your side. I don't want that kind of a problem to pester you either."

She hugged him again, then kissed his cheek.

"You see to that, Sheriff. I just won't allow you to turn up dead." She grinned and ran out the door and half a block down to their house.

Back in the Sagebrush Saloon, Ringo had bought another bottle of whiskey and was doing some serious drinking. He watched the featured attraction of the saloon, a lady singer! She came on the small stage and accompanied herself on an old piano as she sang. Ringo blinked.

He wasn't sure if she were pretty or not. He could see that she had a small waist and good breasts. He shook his head, picked up his bottle and walked with elaborate care out of the saloon toward the best hotel in town where he had already registered. He would finish the bottle in his room. Yes, good idea. Kill the bottle and think about what he was going to do tomorrow.

2

Spur McCoy stepped down from the stage coach at noon the next day, his back sore from the two and a half days of pounding by the coach. Half way he had given up his seat with a backrest to an older woman, changing to her place on the bench in the middle of the stage where there was no back. Sometimes he thought it was easier to ride his own horse than the stage.

He looked around the eastern Oregon town of La Grande. He knew little about it. Cattle mostly, a little bit of timber. Nothing large scale would happen there until the railroad came through.

McCoy stood six-two and weighed a solid two hundred pounds. His reddish brown hair fought with his collar and half hid his ears—when he remembered to get it cut. Green eyes showed over a full reddish brown moustache and long side-burns just a inch this side of mutton chops.

Hidden in his wallet between two other cards pasted together was his identification as a United States Secret Service Agent. Spur called St.

17

Louis his headquarters, and had as his
responsibility the whole western half of the
nation. It was too much, and he was not given
any help. Budgets were tight for manpower they
told him.

Spur was not your usual lawman. He had a
Bachelor of Arts degree from Harvard University
in Boston. He had been an Army Captain during
the big war and an aide in Washington to a U.S.
Senator.

When the Secret Service was established in
1865 he had applied and was accepted as one of
the first agents. Since his was the only federal law
agency that could chase criminals across state
boundaries, that made for more work than they
could possibly manage.

Originally the agency was created to handle one
crime only, counterfeiting. He still worked many
funny money cases, but now everything from
murder to kidnapping to bank robbery was on his
assignment sheet.

He was in La Grande to investigate the death of
a U.S. General Land Office Agent and the destruction of all of his records, files and house. His
wife had been seriously burned in the fire.

William Wood, the director of the agency, had
sent Spur his assignment via telegraph to Portland. It came from General Wilton D. Halleck,
the Number Two man in the agency. It said
simply:

PROCEED TO LA GRANDE ORE AND
INVESTIGATE DEATH OF LAND OFFICE
AGENT JONAS KING. MURDER, ARSON
SUSPECTED. FIND KILLER, PROSECUTE,
RE-ESTABLISH LAND OFFICE IF

POSSIBLE. WIRE UPON COMPLETION YOUR LOCATION.

It was signed by Gen. Halleck, who listed himself as president of Capitol Investigations, Washington D.C.

Spur walked over to the Grande Ronde Hotel with his one big carpet bag and registered. He was in room 202 front looking right down Main Street.

Spur used water from the big china pitcher in his room and gave himself a quick sponge bath. He shaved closely and then dressed in clothes that were not trail dusty and went to see the sheriff. His name was Quincy Younger, and he had been around long enough to know this county inside out.

Sheriff Younger looked at Spur's identification letter with surprise.

"Never even heard of your group," Younger said. "But then that's not unusual. Half the things the Federal Government does never filter down to us way out here anyway. So, what can I do for you?"

"Sheriff, I'm a lawman, the same way you are. I'm here to investigate the death of Jonas King, the man who ran the U.S. Land Office here."

"Yes, Jonas. Terrible tragedy. Fire evidently started about three o'clock in the morning. It was gone before us volunteers got there with our buckets. Someday we'll have a real pumper here to use on fires!"

"Sheriff, we think Jonas was murdered. He wrote his boss in Washington a letter a week before he died. I have a copy of it. He said there had been threats against him. I understand he was also doing the work of the county clerk on a temporary basis."

"Jonas murdered? That's a real surprise. Who would want to do a thing like that to a nice young man like Jonas?"

"I want you to give me some answers to that question. Who in the county could benefit if all the county ownership land records, and the land office records of homesteads and other federal land transactions were wiped out, gone forever?"

"I don't know. We've had considerable home-steading in this valley, some in the mountains. You can homestead a stand of timber just as easy as a river bottom, you know." Younger shook his head. "Benefit? Hell, I don't know. You better talk to the banker. Best one in town is Hirum Follette." He scowled at Spur.

"Can't say I'm too happy knowing that we even *might* have a killer running around town. Course, now that I think more on it, the big ranchers around caused the most uproar about the homesteads. Most of them were grazing public lands they figured they owned, but they didn't. Then a homesteader drops in and fences off his eighty acres and plays all hell with grazing and trail driving."

"Like the RimRock Ranch?"

"The same. But Wade Smith wouldn't do nothing like this. Not murder!"

"Let's hope not." Spur stood to leave. "Oh, and Sheriff, I don't want a word of this to leave this room."

"Yes, yes, I understand. Hirum over at Cattle-man's Bank would be a reliable source for you."

Spur said goodbye and headed for the bank. It was closed. He tapped on the window until someone came. A brief conference through a barely opened front door, and Spur was let in.

Hirum Follette was a short, round man, with fat cheeks, clean shaven and nearly bald. He was not yet forty years old.

After Spur told him the story he paled.

"Oh, God! Not another killing. We have just finished a minor struggle between the big ranchers and the homesteaders. The ranchers got their noses bloody in that one. Served them right; they were dead wrong. They never had title to the land they claimed but wanted to go right on using it."

"Could this tie in? With the records of the county clerk and the land office gone, who can prove they own anything?"

"Copies. All those recordings had to be done in triplicate, with the land owner keeping one copy. Course, more than likely over fifty percent of the owners have lost their copy. They could always get a new one from the County Clerk—up to now."

"Couldn't those owner copies be changed or re-written to include more land than they did originally? Who could disprove it, especially the federal lands through the General Land Bank?"

"Yes, it's a problem, all right."

"Mr. Follette, my job here is to find out who killed Jonas King. Do you have anyone I might begin to talk to? Who would benefit most from this fire?"

"Wade Smith, at the RimRock Ranch, and Travis Odell at the Twin O Ranch. Opposite sides of the county, so they never fight much, but they would like to roust every small rancher and home-steader out of the county."

"Fine, that's a start. What about town people? Any retailer trying to buy up all the property?"

"Not a chance. Nobody is that ambitious."

"Mr. Follette, I would appreciate your not mentioning this to anyone. If it is murder, I want to nail the killer before he knows I'm after him."

The banker agreed and let Spur out the side door. He went down the street two blocks to the edge of the business district to the blackened remains of the U.S. Land Office, and the temporary office of the Wallowa County Clerk. Only a few two by fours stood in one back wall. Nothing had been done to rebuild or clean up the ruins after a month. Some kind of official search had been made, Spur guessed, by the looks of the blackened remains.

But there were no soggy burned masses of paper. When files burn they often singe the edges, burn around the outside, but closely packed paper is not as prone to burning as people think. To burn completely files need to be opened, books must be torn apart, their pages ripped out and the burning remains stirred. He found bindings of the large plat and land ownership books, but none of the pages.

There had been a systematic destruction of the records inside the office before any fire was evident on the outside. No wonder it had taken all night and until three A.M. to finish the job. Jonas could have surprised them, or simply been captured and killed or tied up and left to die when the place caught on fire.

At the far side of the place, away from the street, he found two metal cans. He sniffed them. Coal oil. Each would contain a gallon. Kerosene would be ideal to help burn a building right to the ground. He kicked the cans and wondered what else he should do.

The widow should be next.

He asked at the closest doctor's office. It seemed to be the only one in town, belonging to Dr. William George. The doctor had his office in one wing of his home, and from appearances he had a clinic or small hospital facility in the other section. Spur walked into the office. It was a little after five P.M. and there were three people in the waiting room.

Spur talked to a woman on duty and she said Mrs. King was in the clinic, and yes, he could visit with her for a short time. She was still severely burned, but recovering. The nurse led him through a hall to a hospital-like room.

Mrs. King lay on a bed. She was bandaged over both arms and half of her face. Spur guessed she had many more bandages under the sheet. She smiled with one good eye.

"I am the luckiest person in the world!" she said with an optimistic lilt to her voice. She meant it. "Or maybe the Lord has something else for me to do in this world. Now, how can I help you, young man?"

"Mrs. King, my name is Spur McCoy. I'm interested in the fire at your house. Can you remember anything about what happened that night?"

She blinked back sudden tears, then lifted her brows. "*Remember*. That's about all I can do for another couple of months. It was just a regular day. Jonas often worked late trying to get all the work done. I told him he had two jobs, but he wanted to help out the county until they could get someone reliable. Then too, there was an election coming up in two months to fill the empty post of county clerk.''

"Did he say anything about anyone threatening him, Mrs. King?''

"Threats? In La Grande? My goodness no.''

"Mrs. King. I don't want you to tell anyone, but he sent us a letter to Washington D.C. advising his superiors about threats. We think the fire was deliberately set to destroy all the land records in the county, and that your husband was murdered.''

"Oh, my goodness!''

"Please try and remember anything your husband said that last week before the fire. Anything you can remember will help.''

Her one green eye looked at him with fear, but that quickly changed to anger.

"Yes, Mr. McCoy, I'll certainly remember something!''

"You're a brave woman, Mrs. King. I'll see you later. I hope this hasn't upset you.''

She shook her head but he saw tears growing in her eyes.

Back at the doctor's office, Spur asked to see Dr. George. He said it was official business. The woman showed him into a room and shortly the doctor came in. He was thin, short, with a moustache and thinning hair. He looked to be about fifty, energetic, tired, but friendly.

Briefly Spur introduced himself.

"We think Jonas King was murdered, Doctor. Did you find any marks on the body that might support that theory? I'm scratching for some kind of a lead.''

Dr. George shook his head. He sat down in a chair and took a deep breath. "No, I'm afraid not.

There wasn't enough left to examine. The flesh was almost all burned away, some of the smaller bones had burned. The skull had no bullet holes in it. But that's not much help. There wasn't enough soft tissue left to tell me anything.''

"Not a lot. Oh, Doctor, did you smell anything unusual or foreign to the body when you examined it?''

"Yes, there was something that baffled me. There was a strange odor I always associate with my home at night, or perhaps just as I go to bed.''

"Could it have been kerosene smoke?''

"Oh, my God!, that's it!''

"Kerosene that was poured on the body to make it burn faster?''

"Yes! I should have caught that. Damn them! Then it was murder and arson. Who in this little town could be capable of doing such a thing? We don't have more than four or five hundred people here.''

"I was hoping that you might have some suggestions for me along those lines, Doctor George.''

The doctor shook his head. "I specialize in healing people, making them well again, not in destroying them. But if I get any ideas, I'll be sure to contact you. Where are you staying?''

Spur told him, thanked him and then stepped out into the pre-dusk of the high plains land of eastern Oregon. It had a different feel than the great plains, not as arid as the deserts of the southwest. Somehow a more gentle, softer feel to it. Gentle for everyone but the killer.

3

The tall, slender man who sat in the rocking chair on the far end of the porch at the Grande Ronde Hotel, let the monocle drop from his right eye. It fell on a thin silver chain attached to the watch pocket of his vest. The vest matched the dark blue pin stripe suit. He signalled with his first finger and a man wearing a simple white shirt and blue trousers hurried up to the man in the rocker.

"Yes, Sir Jeffrey?"

"It will soon be time for dinner. Do you know what is on the menu tonight?"

"No, sir. I'll go at once and find out."

"That's a good lad, Edward. Good lad."

The young man of no more than thirty years hurried away toward the hotel's dining room.

Sir Jeffrey Mountbatten watched his man, Edward Long, vanish through the front door of the biggest and best hotel in La Grande. So far, so good, he thought as he watched the people coming and going along the boardwalk of the small western town. It wasn't at all what he thought it would be, but he was ready to accept it as it was—especially when he owned it, even for a short time.

He bowed slightly with a nod to a matron who came up the steps. More and more of the "better" ladies of the town were "just happening" to stop by the Grande Ronde hotel to smile at him, and some were so bold as to come and ask after his good health.

The Americans did go crazy, he thought, when it came to British royalty. They had such outlandish ideas about Lords and Ladies. Sir Jeffrey stood and walked into the lobby, then up to the second floor where he had the three room Presidential suite.

In the hall two matrons smiled at him and they paused.

"Sir Jeffrey," the younger one said. "I wonder if you could tell us about what English ladies wear. I mean do they wear grand gowns all the time?"

She was about twenty, he guessed. She was probably with her mother, a much older woman but still attractive. As she spoke the younger woman turned so he could see the top of her dress which showed a generous portion of cleavage.

He smiled. "Ladies, you both are beautiful and charming. I'm afraid I'm no expert on English women's apparel. However, they do dress almost as nicely as you are now." He paused. "But I must say they are not as cordial and friendly as I find American women. It is most refreshing. It's been delightful talking to you."

"Sir Jeffrey, might I have a word in private with you?" the older woman asked. She was in her forties, a bit stout but with a large bosom.

"Certainly." He moved down the hall a few steps and she followed.

"It's about my daughter. She is a bit shy, but I was hoping that you might be my guest for tea tomorrow, in our rooms here. My daughter, Daisy, is a most engaging girl, and she's interested in getting to know you better." The woman smiled, then went on quickly. "After tea, I would have to leave for an hour or so, and I'm certain that anything you wished to do with Daisy would be all right with her, and me."

"Yes, that's most flattering. However, I do have an inspection ride tomorrow scheduled."

"Oh, well, if you prefer older women, Sir Jeffrey, I should tell you that I'm a widow and truly missing the attentions of a handsome man. Tomorrow would be fine with me as well."

"Thank you, but I'm really afraid I do have this engagement tomorrow. Business, you know. I simply can't avoid it. Perhaps at another time."

"I hope so. I'll be in touch again."

He smiled, bowed slightly and hurried on to the Presidential suite.

When he left Sir Jeffrey on the porch of the hotel, Edward Long slipped out the side door of the hotel and walked down the street to the first saloon. Inside he paid for a nickel beer and mixed, watching poker games and moving closely to several other drinkers.

His nimble fingers worked quickly and when he had two wallets and a soft pull string purse, he faded out the front door and hurried back to the hotel before the men missed their pokes. Once inside the Presidential suite, he closed the door and only then felt safe enough to laugh softly. He had heard about swift Western justice at the end of a rope. Long wasn't sure if that included the small misdemeanor of picking pockets or not.

"Once more I bail you out, *Sir Jeffrey!*" Long said the title and name with elaborate care. He dropped on the bed and took out the billfolds. One had only six dollars in it, and some silver. The other had almost thirty dollars. He untied the soft leather pull string purse with expectation.

"It could be gold!" he said.

Sir Jeffrey came from the other room and stared at the money on the bed. He stepped forward as Long poured out the coins from the soft purse. Long counted the coins with obvious glee.

"Three double eagles, three eagles and some small ones—almost a hundred dollars! Who would be carrying money like that in his pocket?"

"I don't have the foggiest notion, Edward, but he's going to be doubly careful the next time he goes into that saloon. You better not work that one again for a few days." Sir Jeffrey reached for the money, but Long slapped his hand away. "Me dip did the do, so I keep the loot," Long said, dropping into a cockney tinged accent.

"Quite so, old boy. You are excellent at your trade. I have nothing but the utmost respect for you."

Long grinned. "Besides that I'm feeding your arse, as I have for the past two months, ever since Boston. When is this bloody big score going to be coming through that you keep promising me day and night?"

"We start the wheels in motion tomorrow. Within three days half the land owners in Wallowa county will be ready to do business with us."

"Then it's bloody well fifty-fifty, the way we promised?"

"Of course, of course. What could I do without you?"

"Damn little, gov'ner. You're getting me pecker hot again."

Sir Jeffrey smiled and patted the shorter man on the head. "Not until after dinner at least. We should go eat while it's still fashionable."

"Besides, now we have the scratch to pay the bill," Long said.

Dinner was always a time to show off. Long hovered around the great man, making sure he was served properly. When he was settled down to eat, Long slipped away to a back table and ate a steak and all the side dishes.

Lord Mountbatten was bothered by a dozen or more ladies of the town who stopped by to say good evening. Mountbatten loved it. He shyly flirted with each one but offered none the chance to sit down.

By the time dessert was over, Edward Long was hovering around Sir Jeffrey Mountbatten again, acting as his manservant, holding the chair, settling the bill, leaving the tip, doing it all for his master.

An hour later up in their suite, Edward dropped on the bed and laughed.

"It's a bit of fun, laddie, but I'm getting tired of this servant routine. Ain't it about time I get to be the lord again and you the servant?"

"Perish the thought. Not now. We have this whole county just about where we want it. Another two days at the most. Come here and look at this map."

He spread out a large scale map of Wallowa

county which was the north-eastern most in the state, bordering Idaho on one side and Washington on the other.

"We are talking about all those lands that are drained by the Grande Ronde river, the Joseph and the Innaha rivers. That means all of the Wallowa mountains, the big valley of the Grande Ronde and this whole bloody corner of the state. We'll be billionaires!"

"If it works. I think we might have to hit and run fast."

"Not a chance. We've got this one set up so well, planned so completely, that it will roll for at least two months. Think what we can do in two months!"

"And then we take the stage to Portland and vanish in the big city." Edward nodded. "Yeah, it sounds good. I just hope it all works!"

"It can't fail, if you keep up your good work making me look like the bloody duke himself."

Edward snorted. "Bloody, fucking queer duke *you* would make! Where would the bloody next generation come from?"

A knock sounded on the door. Sir Jeffrey vanished in the far room, Edward went to the panel and opened it a foot.

"Eight o'clock, right?" a woman's voice said.

Edward grinned. "Damned if I 'adn't forgotten all about you, love. Come in, come in. Sir Jeffrey has retired for the night in the master bedroom. We won't bother him a bit."

The girl stepped into the room. She was from one of the saloons and had come as promised. She held out her hand. "You're telling me Sir Jeffrey isn't for fucking tonight. I'd really counted on getting my first British nobleman in the old kip."

"Afraid not, love, just me and my little pecker to play with. He's tired out, wouldn't be any sort of fun anyway."

"Too bad. Leastways I'll get me a real Englishman. Be a good change from these farmers and loggers and cowboys." She held out her hand. "That's three dollars, ducks. Three for house calls when there's no duke or earl or prince involved." She laughed. "And I damn well will give you your money's worth."

"You better, ducks," Edward said. "Or I'll bite off one of your nipples!"

Lil giggled. "Oh, you do sound wild and British and all. Do you foreigners do it the way Americans do?"

"Do what?"

"Fuck?"

"We'll have to see. First you show me all the ways you've ever been fucked. Then we'll figure out some new ones for you that are strictly British. Have you ever done the Queen Elizabeth?"

"No, love. Can't say as I have." Lil giggled again and began pulling off her clothes.

"No, sweet one," Edward said. "Slow and easy. I get the fun of unwrapping the package. Now lay down on the bed and look fetching."

In the other room, Sir Jeffrey looked through the two-inch space where he had edged open the connecting door. His face showed a flushed excitement, one hand worked at his crotch and soon his fly came open and he held his stiff penis in his hand. Slowly he began stroking, but he did not watch the girl on the bed, he watched Edward as he slid out of his trousers and dropped bare-assed on the bed.

4

When Spur McCoy left Doctor George's office late that afternoon, he saw a few people looking at him curiously. This was a small town, extremely small, and a stranger stood out here like a peacock in a flock of white leghorns. He shrugged. Strange and curious looks he could live with. He angled across the street and headed along the livery stable on his way to Main Street.

Halfway along the block, a pistol barked from the shadows near the back of the livery. A bullet whizzed over his head and Spur dove toward a thick oak tree that grew near the fence. He peered around the trunk. He saw no one. The shot sounded as if it had come from along the back fence of the livery.

Spur pulled his long barreled Colt and raced along the fence. He saw nothing. He froze against the unpainted boards and listened. Someone was humming *Clementine*. He listened again, then moved slowly toward the sound.

Twenty feet ahead in the weeds beside the fence

sat a man with a six-gun in his lap, and a pint of whiskey in his fist. He didn't hear Spur approach. Spur grabbed the revolver and sniffed it. It had just been fired. He checked it and saw there had only been one round in the cylinder.

The man shook his head and squinted up at Spur.

"I did it! I did it!"

Spur squatted down beside him.

"Yeah, but you missed."

"So what? You said just shoot at him, not hit him." The man tilted the glass bottle again. "Hail, you know I can't hit nothing no more."

Spur took the bottle, threw it against a rock, smashing it, then grabbed the man by the vest and dragged him to his feet.

"We're going for a walk, can you make it?"

"How far to the nearest bar?"

"Not far."

Spur found that the sheriff was not in his office, but a deputy waved at Spur's bushwhacker.

"Know him?" Spur asked the Deputy.

"Sure. That's Park. He's so far down the trail he doesn't even know his name half the time."

"He just took a shot at me."

The deputy took Park's chin in his hand and turned it up to him. "Park, you've been bad again, you know that?"

"Just a little job. Got me a jug and a silver dollar."

"You could have killed this man. Do you realize that?"

"Just one round, never could hit nothing."

The deputy scowled. "Where is your silver dollar?"

"Left it with Lefty at the bar, the Sagebrush

Saloon. He always keeps my money."

The Deputy let him go and turned back to Spur.

"Not much I can do. Park can be hired by any-body in town to try almost anything. The man who hired him could be anybody. Why would somebody try to shoot at you? You're new in town, right?"

"Right, almost six hours, by now. Looking for a somebody I need to find."

"He have a name?"

"Yep, I just don't know it yet. You can have Park. Why don't you dry him out overnight?"

Spur went back to the street. A bar bum, a drunk had taken a shot at him. He hadn't been in town six hours. Did somebody know why he was here, or was it just mistaken identity? This was the first time he'd been in Oregon. Nobody here could know him—unless they recognized him from somewhere else. Entirely possible.

Spur headed for the Sagebrush Saloon. It turned out to be the biggest, noisest bar along Main Street. The Sagebrush had windows across the front, the foot square kind that were cheaper to replace. Dozens of kerosene lamps burned inside.

Most cardsharks liked to gamble at night. The low lighting in gambling halls made it ideal for their bottom dealing and card exchanges. Spur slid through the swinging bat doors and went to the bar.

A man with a white apron around his stomach moved up and eyed Spur. "What's the stranger in town need tonight?"

"A beer and some information."

The apron slid a bottled beer toward him and Spur stopped it.

"Now the question?" the barkeep asked. He was about thirty-five, a little heavy, open and friendly.

"Are you Lefty?"

"Yep."

"Park been in today?"

"Sure, he's always here. Sleeps in back sometimes when I don't catch him."

"Hear he earned a dollar today."

" 'Pears. Leastwise he had one. I kept it for him. A dollar all at once could buy enough rotgut to kill Park."

"You're his banker, or his nursemaid?"

"A little bit of both, but he never has a very big account."

"How did he earn it?"

"Told me he was gonna take a shot at somebody. I warned him not to. As usual he was too drunk to listen."

"He missed me, Lefty." Spur paused to let the message sink in.

"Whoa, none of my doing. I didn't hire him. I'm just his banker. I don't want him to drink himself to death before he's twenty-nine years old."

"And I'd rather he not shoot me even if it is through no fault of his marksmanship. Who hired him?"

The apron waved his hand around the establishment where there were only thirty men and three saloon girls.

"Take your pick. Could have been anyone of these, or anybody in here since we opened when the stage got in at noon." He paused. "Why would somebody want to shoot you? No, that's not right. If they wanted you dead it would have

been a real bushwhacker. Somebody is just trying
to scare you."

"About the size of it. I don't scare easy. I've
only been in town for six hours. I was on that
noon stage."

"Damn peculiar. Anybody know you were
coming?"

"Nobody in town. What else is happening?"

"You've heard of John Ringo?"

"The Texas Terror? He's been in Arizona the
last few years, mostly at Tombstone. Sure, most
people know about Ringo."

"He's in town. Killed a man last night. Sheriff
agreed it was self defense."

"Was it?"

"Yeah. Shot him down right there at the bar.
The dead man went for his gun first. Man! That
Ringo is *fast!*"

"I've heard." Spur thought about it as he took
a pull on the beer.

"Ringo have anything to do with your
problem?"

"How long has he been in town?"

"Came yesterday."

"He's not my worry, then." Spur looked around
and saw the bar filling up.

"Why the sudden trade?"

"In ten minutes our new songbird sings. She's
a looker and she can sing. Full house last night.
She calls herself Colette Paris, whatever that is.
But she can sing."

"When does all this happen?"

"In about five minutes. She sings for a half
hour. Maybe again later if we have enough
customers in the place."

Spur worked on his beer. Who could have been worried about him so quickly? Before he had it figured out a whisper shot around the saloon.

"Ringo!"

The man stood just inside the door, his pair of pearl handled six-guns tied low. He wore range pants, a blue shirt and a brown leather vest.

Ringo scowled at the group around the tables and walked directly to the bar.

"A bottle of that same whiskey," he said. He put three one dollar gold pieces on the bar and took the bottle and glass when the apron set them out. Without another word he walked to a poker game where there was an empty seat, and without asking, sat down.

"Name's John Ringo," he said. "Deal me in."

When the buzzing stopped, the rest of the poker games continued. Somebody plunked on the piano, not a professional, just some cowboy who had taken a few lessons in Milwaukee or Boston or Atlanta, and wished he were home.

A barrage of hoots and yells soon silenced the beginning piano student.

Then the big room was filled with a crashing fanfare on the piano. Spur turned as did everyone else. A small, pale girl in a bright red dress sat at the piano wearing an off the shoulder dress revealing slender arms. She was a brunette with lustrous hair falling halfway down her back and cut straight over her eyes in bangs.

When the fanfare was done she turned to an absolutely quiet house and smiled.

"Good evening, gentlemen, I'm Colette Paris and I'm here tonight to entertain you with some songs, and some piano playing and maybe a memory or two. How many of you remember *The*

Bloody Monogahela?'' She hit a few chords and launched into a tearful ballad about the Civil War.

It was over quickly and she stilled any shouts of one side or the other by charging quickly into *Rosie, You Are My Posy*, and then *My Love is Buried on the Wabash*.

When the three songs were over she stood and bowed and the whole place broke up into a hooting, shouting and clapping uproar of approval. When the applause died down, she smiled and half the men in the place knew she had smiled directly at and for them.

She was a gamine, small and pretty, with a slender body and generous breasts, but it was the sparkle in her eyes and her happy, friendly style that won over her audience.

She did another set of three songs, then asked for requests from the crowd. Quickly came *Old Dan Tucker*, and then *Jimmy Cracker* followed by *Simon Kenton's Revenge*, another song about the Civil War.

Spur sat enthralled by the showmanship of the small girl. He had seen many performers in New York and Washington, but few of them could match this girl who called herself Colette Paris.

Halfway through the next song, John Ringo jumped on the stage and leaned over the piano as she sang. She motioned him away twice, and when he wouldn't leave, she picked up a glass of water from the piano and threw it full in his face.

For a moment there was a shocked, deadly silence, then Ringo roared with laughter, and the shocked and fearful audience joined him. He bowed from the waist and in the sudden silence, doffed an imaginary hat.

"My apologies, Miss Paris. I thought I might have known you in Houston, but I was mistaken." Still chuckling to himself, John Ringo returned to his poker game.

He looked at his whiskey bottle. It was scarcely one quarter gone. Disdaining the glass, he tipped the bottle, lowering the level by an inch and reached for the cards.

"My deal," he said knowing that it wasn't, and challenging anyone at the table to contradict him.

The next few hands went wrong for Ringo. He was a crafty poker player, but luck was not with him, and quickly he lost fifty dollars. The pots were averaging about twenty each until a new player joined the game and the betting picked up.

The next pot was over a hundred. Ringo lost it. He set his mouth firmly and picked up a new hand. Ringo had four nines! On a hand of draw poker he knew that was an extremely good showing. Only a few hands could beat him. Ringo bet his last dollar calling the new player. There was over five hundred dollars in the pot.

The new player now showed that he was a professional gambler. He calmly laid down his hand, four tens.

John Ringo was on his feet in a second, one of his big revolvers drawn before the others could grab a second breath. The muzzle pointed straight at the gambler with the winning hand.

"Cheated!" Ringo thundered. He didn't look to the other men for confirmation. There were no chips at this table, only greenbacks and gold and silver coins.

Ringo looked at the four men around the table. They made no move. The gambler stared at the muzzle and shook his head slowly.

"Mr. Ringo. I did not cheat. However, if you want the pot so badly, why don't you take the money? If you'll excuse me I'll be going back to my hotel." The gambler stared at Ringo for five seconds, then calmly turned his back and began to walk away from the table.

There was hardly a sound in the saloon except the man's footfalls.

Ringo watched him a moment, then looked down at the pot on the table that held more than five hundred dollars. It was two years wages for the average working man. Ringo reached for the money with his left hand. The gambler spun suddenly, his right hand pulling a .32 caliber hideout gun with a two inch barrel from his pocket. He had it drawn but not aimed when Ringo fired his .44. The round went through the gambler's heart, slamming him backwards on the top of a poker table, smearing the cards and the money with blood as he skidded off, hit the plank floor and died.

Ringo held his gun on the man for a moment, heard the rush of air from his lungs in a death rattle, then holstered his .44, picked up the money on the table and walked out the door.

The barkeep quietly sent a flunky out the back way to get the sheriff.

Colette came to the bar to talk to the barkeep, who it turned out also owned the place. They talked for a few minutes, and she nodded. Then she turned to Spur who still stood there.

"Miss Paris, you sing extremely well," Spur said.

"Thank you." She smiled. "You're from the east, Boston?"

"I went to school there and picked up a trace of

that accent."

"I thought so. I come from Portland, Maine."

"Could I buy you a drink?"

"No, no thanks. I'm to do another show later on. I must keep a clear head. Now I need to rest." She paused. "You know my name, but I don't know yours." She was frank, open, friendly.

"Spur McCoy, Miss. I'm staying at the Grande Ronde Hotel."

"Nice to meet you, Mr. McCoy. Perhaps I'll see you again. I'm at the same hotel." She turned then and went behind the bar to what was probably an office or private quarters.

Spur lifted his brows.

The barkeep/owner smiled. "A nice lady. She is not to be confused with our saloon girls."

"That would hardly be possible," Spur said. He paid for his second beer, finished it and headed for his hotel. He took a roundabout route, staying in the shadows, backtracking, and watching his back trail.

No one was following him. Five minutes later he eased into his hotel room and lit the lamp. A long white envelope lay on the floor just inside the door where someone had slipped it under the door while he had been gone.

Spur locked the door, then picked up the envelope.

5

Spur tore open the envelope. A piece of purple, scented stationery came out. On it in a dainty feminine hand he saw the message.

"Mr. Spur McCoy. You could help me. I need your aid. Please come to Room 215 as soon as possible."

There was no signature.

Spur read the note again. It certainly didn't look like a set-up. Still, someone had hired a drunk to take a shot at him, to scare him. How could a purple, scented stationery using woman hurt him? It would be the man in the closet or in the hall or waiting in a room with a connecting door who could do the damage.

And it could be a lead to a killer.

He checked his appearance, combed his hair and brushed back his moustache, then put his clip on holster in his boottop with the hideaway derringer and went down the hall. Room 215 was on the same floor as his. He found it, surveyed both ends of the hall, but saw no one move. He heard nothing. Gently he knocked on the door.

It opened at once.

The girl standing there was tall, maybe five-seven, her hair was light blonde and had been cut short. Huge brown eyes gazed at him and a smile lit up her pretty face. She wore a dress buttoned to her chin and wrists.

"Oh, Mr. McCoy! I'm so glad you got my note. I missed you at supper. Please come in."

Spur had left his hat in his room. He took one more look up and down the hall, then stepped inside.

"Yes, I am Spur McCoy. And who might you be?"

"You can call me Maggie. I live here. I fix my room any way that I want to." She spun around like a school girl. "Isn't this a nice room?"

"Indeed it is, Maggie. You said you needed some help."

"Oh, yes. I'm just so bored and unhappy and sad, that I think I might just take my own life. You wouldn't want that to happen, would you? So what I decided when I saw you get off the stage, was that you could help me. It isn't hard, and if you're short of money, I can even—you know—help pay your hotel bill or whatever."

She saw him look up quickly.

Maggie shook her hand in front of him when he saw how forcefully he reacted to that idea. "No, forget about that, but I do need your help desperately. I get so depressed and I really don't want to shoot myself, although I do have a gun, a .32 caliber I think it is, and that would be plenty enough to kill me."

Spur frowned. "This sounds more like you need a doctor, maybe Dr. George. He would know what to do more than I would."

"Oh, no, no! I can't go to him. I've known him all my life and it wouldn't be the same. Don't you see, I need someone I've just met to talk to, so I can tell you all my problems and worries and you won't laugh at me."

"I would never laugh at such a pretty lady," Spur said.

"There! See what I mean? I feel better already. You just said I was pretty. Now Dr. George would never tell me that, right? So you have to stay and help me. I want you to tell me all about yourself, just as if . . . as if you were here courting me. Then I can tell you about myself, and I'll feel just ever so much better."

"I'm afraid this isn't my usual line of work, Maggie. Now if you'll excuse me, I really should get back to my room."

"No! you can't go or I'll kill myself! I will!" She darted to the dresser and brought out a business-like .32 caliber revolver. She pointed it at him without putting her finger on the trigger. Spur could see that there were lead slugs showing through the end of each cylinder.

He changed his attitude, held up both hands, and sat in the room's one straight backed chair. There also were two other upholstered chairs, and a table at one side. The bed was on the far side. He realized the room was at least twice as large as his own. It must face the alley.

"Good." I'll put this horrid thing away. I really don't want to use it, you know."

She sat on the bed facing him. "Now, what shall we talk about? You first."

"What about your family, Maggie? Can't you talk to them?"

Her face turned sad. "Yes, I wish I could. They died, my mother and father and a brother. Indians. It was terrible. A year ago now. But I'll never forget it." She shook her head and her face brightened. "Now, Mr. McCoy. Tell me about yourself." As she said it she unbuttoned her dress at her wrists.

"Oh, you don't mind, do you? It is a little warm in here." She undid her wrists and rolled the sleeves back, then undid the buttons at her throat but only three or four. "Now, what about you, Mr. McCoy?"

"I come from New York City, where I went to school. My father owns a store there."

"How exciting! Are there really all those people living in one place, in one town?"

"Yes, I should say. Almost two million people in the city. It's really like a lot of little cities all pushed together."

"So many people." As she said it, she undid more of the buttons at her throat, they extended all the way to her waist.

She undid two more buttons.

"Tell me how it was to grow up with all those neighbors." she laughed. "Goodness, around here we have three hundred people and sometimes it seems tremendously crowded."

Again she undid more of the buttons.

"So what kind of a business does your father have?"

"He has several, really," Spur said. At first Spur thought she was just opening a few of the buttons down the front, now she kept moving her fingers, and the buttons opened lower and lower. He could see white fabric showing through the opening.

"Maggie . . ."

She smiled. "Spur McCoy, am I embarrassing you? They're just buttons. I'm still entirely covered. See." She spread apart the front of her dress and the white chemise was indeed covering her breasts.

"Really, Maggie, I don't think . . ."

"Hush, Spur McCoy. I told you I need you. I do. I'm going to show you just how much I need you." She shrugged out of the top of her dress, then in one quick move lifted the chemise over her head. She sat there calmly, bare now to the waist, her breasts still bouncing slightly from her motion.

The twin peaks were still pointed with youth, creamy white and tipped with soft pink areolas and small darker nipples. Before he could move, she scrambled forward and sat on his lap. She put her arms around his neck and kissed his cheek, then nibbled at his lips.

"Spur, darling Spur McCoy! I need you desperately. Don't you understand? Do I have to say it? Please, darling Spur!"

Spur groaned softly.

Maggie giggled. Her hand moved down by her hips and she touched his erection which was growing by the second.

"I can feel part of you who is glad to see me all bare. Do you like my titties?"

Spur could stand it no longer. He bent and kissed her breasts, then licked her nipples, slowly at first, than faster and faster as he saw them grow and enlarge. He held off as long as he could, then he sucked one of her luscious mounds into his mouth, and chewed and licked and ate her as Maggie moaned low in her throat and her hand rubbed at his crotch.

"Christ, we better at least lock the door," Spur said.

"I'll do it," Maggie said. She jumped off his lap, pushed him out of the straight chair and forced the back of it under the door knob and tilted, angled out resting only on the rear two legs. Then she took a key and locked the door and turned the key half a turn to leave it in the keyhole so no master key could be used.

Her breasts bounced and swayed and jiggled as Spur watched, his pressure building.

She came to him, and he lifted her off her feet, kissing her open mouth, his own mouth exploring hers as deeply as he could. She wiggled to be put down. Quickly she slid out of the dress, then four petticoats slipped away until she wore only billowy pink underpants that came to her knees. She jumped on the bed and patted the spot beside her.

"Now it's my turn to undress you," She said.

"Be gentle with me," Spur said and she laughed at him, then took off his vest and town shirt and marveled at the black hair on his chest. She toyed with it, tried to braid it, then kissed it and played with his man breasts.

His boots came next and then his pants. She stared in anticipation at the bulge in his short underpants, and when she pulled them down, she sat back and stared in frank admiration.

"I still don't understand how it can get so hard and stiff that way, and then just moments later he can be so tiny and short and soft."

"It's known as rising to the occasion," Spur said, enjoying himself. It was nice to be the one being seduced for a change. She pulled his underwear off his feet and sat on his stomach. Then slowly she bent over him until her breasts hung enticingly inches away from his mouth.

"Want a bite of a sweet cookie? I have chocolate on the right, and vanilla on the left."

He compromised by licking and chewing both.

She wiggled with delight, her still covered crotch dropping and grinding against his erection. She rolled over and pulled down the pink silk undergarment, then kicked it across the room.

She came to her knees beside him, her legs spread, the pink wetness of her slit showing past a brush of blonde curls. Slowly she pumped her hips forward, her crotch coming almost to his face as the opening puckered and opened.

She kissed his mouth hard and pulled away quickly.

"Darling Spur, I have three holes, which one do you want first? We're going to do all three tonight, I promise you!"

"You pick," he said, sitting up. She kissed his mouth again, then his chin and his neck, worked down a string of hot kisses cross his chest and his little belly and through the black hair around his crotch.

"First," she said, and slid her mouth around his pulsating penis.

Spur groaned with delight, his hips pumped upward and she sucked him in her mouth, gurgling as she pumped up and down. He came out of her mouth, rolled her over and knelt stradling her shoulders as she lay flat on her back. He slowly bent forward, inserting himself into her mouth. Her eyes went wide, then she nodded and took him as he provided the motion, gentle at first, pumping in and out of her mouth.

Sweat beaded her forehead. She moaned in joy as he worked faster and faster. Spur had always had a special feeling for making love this way. It meant a special commitment by the woman and he never forced one. But when she offered . . .

He felt the urgency building. Deep down the seeds of new life were stirring. Then he felt them surging forward, the undeniable journey had started. He groaned and bellowed in expectation as the pulsating came closer and closer. Then with one final surge he shouted six times, one for each spurt as he emptied himself and at the same time sensed she was swallowing and sucking at him.

He heaved once more and lifted away from her, rolling over on his back, panting like a steam engine gushing out hot breath and dragging in new air to feed his starved cells.

She snuggled against him, taking one of his hands and cupping it around her breast. He massaged her mound gently and she purred.

"Was that good?" she asked.

"Great, the best ever. You are marvelous. How did you learn to be so good?"

"Nobody has to learn, it's natural. Everyone can fuck good. How else would we have so many people? Nobody teaches the animals. I've seen them on the ranches."

They both laughed. Then she took his hand and brought it down to her crotch. "Do me," she said softly.

"What?"

"Rub me, play my little guitar, strum me! Make me go out of my mind!"

She put his finger on her clit and he explored a moment, found the right spot and began twanging her. After only a dozen strokes she was wailing and pumping her hips against him. Then she screeched softly, and he saw that she had her face in the pillow. Her whole body rattled and vibrated like an earthquake, shaking like she was going to come apart. She gasped and shivered.

Slowly her wails into the pillow slacked off, and her hips slowed in their tattoo against him. At last she reached down and pulled his hand away from her and gave a long, slow sigh before she reached up and kissed his cheek.

"It's so much better when a man does me that way," she said, then she heaved a sigh and went to sleep. Her face still had a soft smile on it.

Spur lay there holding her in his arms as she slept. He grinned, afraid to move, not wanting to awaken her. At last he moved slightly and she awoke and sat up. She watched him a minute, then grinned.

"Don't mind me," she said. I always nod off for a minute after I have a good one. You did me just great!" She laughed at the surprise on his face. Slowly she reached over and kissed him, then her hands were busy at his crotch. Her hands had a marvelous effect on him.

"Come on, Big Boy, you've had enough rest. It's playtime again, playpen time. The choices are now down to two."

Spur leaned back, put his hands under his head and relaxed. It was going to be a great night, and this was only the start. If somebody was planning on blowing him into pieces tonight in his bed, they would have a surprise. This was the best defensive move he had made since coming to town, and certainly the one that he had enjoyed the most.

Unless, of course, Maggie was the one who wanted to blow his brains out.

6

Spur had always thought of himself as a light sleeper. In the wilderness he would wake up if an Indian came within a hundred yards of his camp.

He had to rethink his ability the next morning when he woke up about six A.M. and the tall blonde with the short cut hair was gone from the room. She was not only gone, she had moved out. Nothing that was hers seemed to still be there, but his clothes, his guns and his purse were untouched.

Spur got back to his own room, shaved and dressed in his town clothes, a clean shirt and lightweight doeskin brown vest and dark brown pants. He gave up on the string tie and went down for breakfast when the dining room opened at seven.

Maggie was not there. Strange. Interesting girl, but a little on the weird side. She had been delightful when it came to making love.

Right after a stack of buckwheat cakes and syrup covered with three sunnyside-up eggs,

Spur went to see a man represented as the best lawyer in town. His name was Irvin Dunlap, and he had been practicing law in La Grande since the area became a territory back in 1848.

A wooden ramp led up the two steps into the lawyer's office. Spur went in and talked with a young law clerk who said Mr. Dunlap was busy, but he would be free to consult with Spur in ten minutes. Spur took a walk up and down the three block long business district, noticing nothing unusual or different from most frontier towns. The people were a bit more friendly, he decided, but that was about it.

Back in the law office, Spur walked into the private room and found Irvin Dunlap sitting in a wheel chair. He introduced himself, shook hands and grinned.

"Been several people wondering about you, Mr. McCoy. If I had to guess, I'd say you were a Federal man interested in what happened to the General Land Office and all those records."

Spur laughed. "Remind me to get you to defend me in Oregon if I ever have the need," Spur said. "You're partly right, Mr. Dunlap. I am interested in those records. For example, I have a long time deed to property up the valley a ways, but I've lost my piece of paper. How do I prove it's mine?"

"Be damn hard. I'm trying to put together some stopgap procedures such as filing of affidavits by at least six unrelated individuals who will swear as to ownership and approximate boundaries."

"Stopgap sounds right. Who settles disputes?"

"We haven't got that far yet. I'm trying to work with the state legislature and the state's attorney general. It's all up in the air."

"Heard anything from the Land Grant people in Washington?" Spur asked.

"I notified them of the fire, nothing else. If you're from there you're the first one."

"They at least should have records in Washington D.C. of all land grant activity, homesteads, leases, land sales. Or do they?" Spur was puzzled.

"We think so. But frankly, Mr. McCoy, by the time any such proof gets here, we could have a land fight that will rank right next to the Civil War."

"Who in the county stands to benefit most by the destruction of the records, Mr. Dunlap?"

"Ah ha! The true colors start to show. Figured you were Federal but I just didn't have any idea in what capacity. Now I've got it pegged. You're enforcement. You're here to find out who set the place on fire, and how Jonas was killed. At least I have that worked out."

"Right, Mr. Dunlap, but I'd appreciate your not spreading it around. I suppose you know that the records were not just burned, they were *systematically destroyed* by burning. You may have tried to burn paper, packed together paper. It's hard to burn it up completely unless it is stirred around and separated."

"Agreed. I took a look at the remains over there, too."

"So who will be the big winner?"

"The ones who always win, the entrenched, well established land owners. Cattle ranchers, the timbermen who are just waiting for a railroad to cut through here so they can get their lumber shipped out. Those are the big winners. They can bloat their ownership by hundreds of thousands of acres and no one can say that they are over-stating the truth. This could be a headache, a morass of conflict and lawsuits for generations.''

"RimRock Ranch?"

"Of course, the largest in the county and the other huge one, the Twin O Ranch run by Travis Odell. Both outfits have ownership of about five thousand acres. But, like others, they have been grazing public lands so long they sometimes think it's theirs. Now I don't know where the homesteaders will settle down. How can they tell what's left to homestead?"

Dunlap rolled in his chair to the window and looked out on Main Street.

"Damn, I wish this hadn't happened. Without those records a lot of people are going to lose what little they own. We're going to see the biggest case of land grab greed that's ever taken place. And I don't have a prayer of an idea how to stop it." He shook his head, then rolled back.

"Frankly, I've been expecting you. I've got a letter for you here to Judge Farley Inglesia. He's the circuit court judge making his rounds, and he's here for two more days. Take this over to the county office where we have our one court room, and see if you can talk to him. In this letter are my suggestions for putting the stopgap plan into action.

"Talk to Judge Inglesia. He's a smart man, and a fair one. He might have some ideas."

Spur tried. A law clerk took the letter to the judge along with Spur's invitation to dinner. He had to eat after the morning session. Ten minutes later the clerk came back with a handwritten note.

"Dear Mr. McCoy. I must work through my

noon meal. I can tell you nothing more about the local land record problem. Mr. Dunlap is the local expert. Go with his suggestions. Good luck in your work."

Spur changed plans, had a quick bowl of soup at a cafe and went to the La Grande Stables. He rented a horse and saddle, and a 7-shot Spencer repeating rifle. Then he got directions to the RimRock Ranch, and turned the big roan upstream along the Grande Ronde river.

The stable man told him it was about eight miles to the ranch. It took Spur two hours to ride there, including the time he got lost. He could see the big overhead archway type gate at the ranch just off the main trail. He turned that way and saw a rider swing away from a cluster of cattle and ride to meet him.

"Howdy," the ranch hand said.

"Afternoon," Spur said. "This the RimRock Ranch spread?"

"Peers as how."

"Good. I need to talk with Wade Smith."

"He's up at the main ranchhouse. I'll be glad to show you the way."

Spur wasn't sure if it was an escort or a guard who rode with him, but both purposes were served. The man led him to a wide veranda that looked out on the Grande Ronde river less than a quarter of a mile away.

A small, heavyset man with arms as thick as cedar fenceposts worked over a battered oak desk. He looked up as they came on the veranda.

"Mr. Smith, you have a visitor," the hand said.

"Thanks, Bert," Smith said. He stood and held out a rope and rein in a gnarled right hand. "Smith is my name," he said.

"Mr. Smith. I'm Spur McCoy." They shook.

"Yep, heard you were in town. Got to be something to do with the Land Office, right?"

"That's one of the things I like about a small community, Mr. Smith. Actually I'm not from the Land Office."

"Oh. Well, fine. What can I do for you?"

"Do you know who killed Jonas King?"

"Killed? I thought it was an accident?"

"That's what the killer wanted everyone to think. The fires got so hot so quickly he didn't have a chance to take away two gallon cans that had been filled with coal oil. Also, Dr. George told me that the burned body had the odor of kerosene on it, and the residual matter from burned kerosene as well. Someone deliberately poured the fluid on the body to burn it beyond recognition."

"Who the hell would do that?" Wade Smith asked. "Certainly not me, or any of my hands."

"Mr. Smith, who would benefit most if all of the county and federal land records for the county were destroyed?"

"The biggest land owners in the county. Me and Travis Odell."

"Exactly. Without those records, proof of ownership could be in the courts for twenty years in this county. We need to do something about it."

"And the rich get richer. As well as homesteading would come to a halt," Wade Smith said. "Nobody would know what land was available."

"Which would never make a big rancher angry. Mr. Wade, I want to enlist your help."

"Hell no! I ain't gonna help tie the noose to

hang myself with. Not a chance in hell! You come out here and practically tell me I'm suspect in a killing, and then tell me you want me to find out who did it. Hell no! Now you get yourself off my spread before I sic one of my boys on your tail. You rode on here nice and peaceful. Now you go get on your horse and you ride off the same way."

"I'm not accusing you of anything, Mr. Smith."

"Daddy?" a woman's voice came from the door into the house. A woman stood there, looking into the veranda. "Daddy, I thought I heard another voice. I just don't understand this at all. You should have told me we had company."

Spur turned, the voice vaguely familiar. When the woman came in the light of the porch he saw the tall, slender form, then the short blonde hair. Maggie! She was the same girl who had invited him to her room and into her bed last night! She smiled formally at him and looked at her father with more than a little touch of impatience.

"You could introduce us, Father."

"No sense, Mr. McCoy was just leaving."

"Oh, Mr. McCoy." She held out her hand. "It's nice to meet you, Mr. McCoy. I'm Margaret Smith."

Spur was jolted by the surprise. From naked in bed with her ten hours ago to this formal introduction was such a surprise that it was almost more than he could believe. But she was the same woman. The short blonde hair, direct, piercing brown eyes, and the quick smile. He even knew how she looked under her cool blue dress.

"Mr. McCoy, we get visitors so seldom, I do hope that you can stay to supper."

"No, Margaret. I told you, Mr. McCoy is just

leaving. There's no cause for you to be here."

Spur at last found his voice.

"Yes, Miss Smith, I'm sorry, but I do have business back in town. Perhaps I could invite you to supper sometime at the hotel. I hear they have some excellent dishes."

"Oh, I'm sorry. I don't get into town much."

"Good bye, Mr. McCoy," Wade Smith said sharply. "A shame you had the long ride for nothing."

"Quite to the contrary, Mr. Smith. I have learned a lot. I'll be talking with you later." he turned to Margaret. "Miss Smith, that supper invitation is open any time. I'm staying at the Grande Ronde Hotel."

He turned and walked out of the house. Margaret started to follow, but a curt command by her father stopped her. By then Spur was off the veranda.

Spur's horse was where he had left it. The rider who brought him in was waiting to escort him out to the gate. Spur noticed that the man had a six-gun on his left hip and a Winchester in his boot. The man was a guard after all. They said little as they rode to the gate.

They had just passed the gate, when the cowboy held up his hand and they both stopped. The man eyed Spur with more than a little anger.

"Mr. Smith has a message for you, big man. He says don't come back on RimRock Ranch land again, unless you're asked. And don't under any circumstances try to see or talk to his daughter. He wants you to understand them two points real good. You do understand them?"

"Yes, understood. Now, I have a message for Mr. Smith. You tell him I'll go on anybody's land where I think I need to go, and my two buddies, Mr. Spencer and Mr. Colt, will be with me. As far as his daughter goes, that will be strictly up to the lady. Whatever she wants to do is fine with me.''

Spur turned and rode away.

He was two miles from the ranch gate, just riding down into a low spot where the trail wound near to a bend in the Grande Ronde River, when a rifle shot jolted into the quiet countryside. Spur heard the flutter of the air as the round passed within two feet of him. He dove off the horse to the left and rolled toward some rocks left exposed by the river at flood stage. It was two feet high.

Two more rifle shots sent hot lead toward him. One round went over the rocks, the second hit the granite and shattered. Spur looked around the rock and saw the faint trails of blue gunpowder smoke two hundred yards to the left, slightly above him in a heavy stand of pine. Two more shots sounded and the bullets sang overhead.

He was pinned down. There was no place to move to that would give him any protection. All the bushwhackers had to do was work around behind him and shoot him full of lead!

7

Spur ducked as a rifle round sang off the rock and careened away into the high plateau of Eastern Oregon. He had just been shot at from ambush. He dove off his horse and now evaluated his situation. One gun or two out there? He figured two. They had the high ground and cover. He had a six-gun and not much to go on.

His rifle! He had to have the Spencer or they could circle around and cut him to pieces. His roan mare stood munching on spring grass ten yards toward the trees. The Spencer rested in the boot on Spur's side of the mount. With three strides he could put the horse between himself and the rifles on the slope.

There was nothing else to think about. Spur leaped to his feet, boots churning the ground as he darted to his horse, grabbed the reins and ran with the big roan mare. She half dragged him but he kept up with her by jerking back on the reins. With one hand, he pulled the Spencer from the boot and kept running.

Three shots sounded and he felt one tick his boot as he ran. Then a fourth shot came and the mare bellowed in rage and stumbled. She crashed into Spur, spinning him away as she fell, rolling once, scrambling to her feet and galloping straight downstream as fast as she could go.

Spur shook his head, rolled and came into a crouch, the Spencer still in his left hand, his right checking the six gun to be sure it was still holstered.

Dirt spurted in front of him from a rifle slug. He darted the other way, got his bearings and rushed twenty feet to the side of the river where the stream had cut a six-foot gorge in the land that was now a dry former water course.

He dove the last six feet as four more rifle shots sprayed around him. He rolled over the lip and fell to a ledge and scrambled to his feet. He was out of sight, and unhurt.

Spur knew the mare had moved downstream. He could get her later. He was more interested in identifying at least one of the men bushwhacking him. He ran upstream where the gully swung close to the pine grove.

Five minutes later he was out of the dry stream bed and into the timber. He moved swiftly now, taking care not to make any noise as he ran through the typical eastern Oregon pine woods. There was little brush, almost no hardwoods, just the pines growing straight and tall.

After moving fifty yards forward, he stopped and peered around a two-foot thick Ponderosa. Ahead he could hear someone talking. He made sure the rifle had a round in the chamber and was ready to fire, then he ran with the weapon at high port, gliding from one tree to the next, moving toward the voices.

Another twenty yards ahead he paused. He could see through a slight clearing to the fringe of trees along the edge of the grove. Two men lay along the downslope watching the river.

"Hell, he's long gone by now," one said.

"Not a hindtail chance. He's the kind who comes after guys who hurt him, and we hurt him. He's on foot. Ain't nothing makes a cowboy madder than a wet hen than to have to walk. He'll be coming."

"You watching our arse-end backside?"

"Now and then."

Spur slid to the ground and lifted the Spencer. He sighted in on the closest man and his finger began to tighten on the trigger. He wanted to blast both of them straight into hell, but he relaxed. He was a lawman.

McCoy kept the man in his sights and yelled out his warning.

"Don't move either one of you, I've got you covered. You're both under arrest."

At the first words, one man rolled out of sight behind a log. The second one tried the other direction but there was no cover. Spur slammed two shots at him as he moved, the second one plunged into his stomach, slanted upward through his lung and cut his heart in half.

Spur was up and running. The second man had vanished. A moment later Spur heard the sound of hooves on the soft pine woods floor and the second bushwhacker rode off through the trees. There was no chance for even one shot.

The Secret Agent went back to the first man and checked him. He was dead. Spur found the man's horse where it had been left and brought it back. He tied the dead man over the horse just behind the saddle, mounted and rode for town.

He found his roan mare a mile down the river munching on new grass. She had a bullet crease across her rear quarters, but was not hurt seriously. She let him ride up and tie her reins to his saddle.

There was no chance to identify the man who got away, but someone in town should know this one.

An hour later, Spur tied up both horses at the sheriff's office. Half a dozen men gathered round the deadman. The sheriff came out, glanced at Spur, then went to the corpse and lifted the head so he could see his face.

"Tex Abbot. Been around town for a year or so. Works now and again as a ranch hand. Never been steady with any spread. Heard he was good with his six-gun. Guess he wasn't good enough." The sheriff told one of the gawkers to take the body over to the undertaker, and motioned Spur inside.

Spur told the story to a grim sheriff.

"Far as I know, Wade Smith could have sent him after me, told him to wait until I got off the RRR land and fill me with lead."

"Not likely. Smith don't go for Texans, likes to keep his crew all northerners. Besides, he never uses part timers. He hires on a hand, he stays on year round."

Spur sighed and stood up. "You do the paper and I'll sign it, Sheriff. This don't help me much on my problem. Oh, the horse and saddle were his. That should pay for his burying. I got to get my nag back to the livery."

The dead man helped little. If Spur had

wounded him he could have made him tell who hired the pair. Damnit!

He couldn't help but think about Maggie Margaret Smith. She must sneak into town for a fling now and then. It was obvious that her father kept a tight rein on her. When she got the chance to come to town she let out all of her frustrations. He wondered why she wasn't married and settled down. But he knew. No one in the area was "good enough" for Wade Smith's darling.

Spur went to the doctor office where he talked with the widow King again. She was sitting up now and some of the bandages were gone from her face. Her right hand had not been burned but the rest of that arm was still covered.

"Mr. McCoy, I've been remembering things. Jonas told me he was worried about something and was going to write a letter to Washington D.C. He never said what it was about."

"We got the letter, it has helped. That's why I'm here."

"Good. That night of the fire, I remember that Jonas was working late. He said he had some more county work to do. He was looking forward to the special election to name a new county clerk. The former one got so sick he had to quit."

Spur handed her a glass of water. She went on.

"That night I kept hearing people talking. It wasn't all that late, but people did come to do business at night when they saw Jonas working. But when I woke up much later, I could smell something. It was kerosene! The whole upstairs seemed to smell of kerosene. Then the flames came and I had to run down the stairs. That's when I got burned. Could it have been kerosene?"

"Yes, Mrs. Jonas. We're convinced that someone deliberately set the fire, and they also killed your husband. It wasn't just an accident."

"Oh no!" tears seeped from her eyes onto the bandages.

"I'm sorry, Mrs. King. I'm going to bring them to justice. Is there anything else you remember about that night?"

"No, but that was the same day that the Englishman came in. He wanted a map of the county and thought it would be free. Jonas said he was rude, not at all like he imagined a titled Englishman should behave."

"An Englishman. How long has he been in town?"

"Maybe a month or so. Jonas said the talk is that he's looking for a cattle ranch to buy. But mostly he sits in the hotel or on the veranda watching the people walk by."

"Interesting. Mrs. King, do you remember your husband saying anything about disputes over land ownership lately? Did anyone come in for copies of his deed to prove ownership?"

She shook her head. "Not recently."

Spur thanked her, said goodbye and went to the hotel for a change of shirt, and then supper in the dining room. He had completely missed his noon feeding time somehow.

After supper, Spur smoked a long, thin, black cigar as he sat on the veranda and watched the sun go own. He had thought through the case but had little more to go on. The big ranchers were still the ones who would profit most by the land records problem.

He gave up on it and went to the Sagebrush Saloon for a drink. The singer, Colette Paris came by and sat at his table.

She smiled at him. "I hope you don't mind. I just had to get out of that little dressing room, they gave me. I'm not due to go on for another half hour. I could use a sarsaparilla. Anything else is hard on my voice."

Spur went to the bar and brought her back one of the carbonated, non-alcoholic drinks. "It's a beautiful voice. How come you're doing the Wild West circuit?"

"Reasons. Partly because I got tired of the eastern cities and the crazy people who live there."

"Except New York," Spur said.

She laughed. "Yes, except New York."

"How long will you be here?"

"A week, maybe two weeks. Depends how long Lefty can keep on making money with me. When he starts losing money, I move on to the next town."

"Pendleton," Spur said remembering the next little town toward Portland.

"Wherever, it really doesn't matter."

"You don't have a husband or a fiance somewhere, then?"

"No."

Before she could elaborate, John Ringo came into the saloon. Everyone knew at once that John had arrived.

"Where the hell's the big money action in this town? I want to play me some goddamned poker!"

He looked around, saw Colette and barged up to the table. He ignored Spur, looked at Colette and sat down quickly.

Spur could see the man was drunk, but this one

was more dangerous and a better shot drunk than sober.

"Well, if it ain't the little pussy who threw her drink in my face. Now that ain't nice. Didn't your mamma ever tell you that? But, what the hell, we'll forget all about that. Why don't we dance?"

"There isn't any music."

"Then get the piano player to play something. Have him play *Harvest Moon's Courting Time*. I like that one."

"We don't have a piano player here."

"Damnit! why not? Hell, we'll just go upstairs and I'll unwrap your pretty little package and we'll have a wild time in bed."

"You must be out of your mind. Get away from me!"

John Ringo laughed, stood, swept the small girl up in his arms as she hit him with her small, ineffectual fists.

"Now, calm down little hellcat. Enough time to do all that when I'm laying on top of you."

Spur stood and faced Ringo. "Put her down, John. The lady isn't going anywhere."

Ringo focused on Spur, seeing him for the first time. "Shut up, asshole! This is none of your business. Go fuck yourself!"

Spur swung his right fist with all his two hundred pounds behind it. Ringo had no way to defend himself. The big fist collided with his jaw, powering him backwards. His hands sagged, dropping Colette. Spur jumped forward and caught her just before she hit the floor. He was back on his feet in seconds.

But there was no fight left in John Ringo. He sat on the floor holding his jaw, then he began to weave and fell on his face on the planks.

Spur stood up Colette and knelt beside Ringo. He pulled his hands behind him and tied Ringo's wrists together with a length of rawhide he took from his pocket.

"Go get the sheriff," Spur said, snapping the order to a man standing nearby. The man stood up straighter as if he had been in the Army.

"Yes sir!" he said and ran out the front door.

Spur rolled John Ringo over. He was still unconscious. Spur picked up a half filled mug of beer from the table and poured it in the outlaw's face.

Ringo came to sputtering and swearing. When he saw he was on the floor and his hands tied he screamed in fury.

When he quieted, Spur knelt beside him. "Ringo, you're drunk and you're going to jail."

"What for?"

"Drunk and disorderly, and assault and battery on a female."

"Didn't hit her. What the hell you mean? She's a fucking saloon girl!"

Sheriff Younger came in and scowled down at Ringo. The county lawman motioned Spur to one side. "What the hell you doing? I'm hoping Ringo will ride out of here in a day or two. What did he do?"

Spur told Sheriff Younger. "You jail him now, or I'm swearing out a warrant for him myself. Take your pick."

Younger shrugged. "Help me get him to a cell. And you better be there tomorrow when I let him out. I'll hold him overnight, but after that he's gonna be gunning for your hide, not mine. I'll make that damn plain."

"I bet you will, Sheriff. You're all guts. Let's

get him into a cell and then worry about it."

Just before they led Ringo out of the place, Colette touched Spur's arm. "Thank you, Spur McCoy," she said softly. "I owe you, and I am a person who always pays my debts."

Spur touched his hat and led John Ringo to jail.

8

Sir Jeffrey Mountbatten sat at the small table in the suite of rooms at the Grande Ronde hotel. Half of it was covered with books, and papers and directly under the lamp lay a document with fancy borders and scrolled work that looked as if it had all been done by hand with a quill pen.

Sir Jeffrey picked it up and a look of awe covered his face.

"It's beautiful! Magnificent. The man who did this was really a great artist. He probably painted nights and holidays on his 'better quality work' which never sold. These certificates he made for a living. Extraordinary!"

Edward Long lounged on the couch in the middle room of the suite, the sitting room. He was buried in a dime novel featuring "Wild Zack and His Daring Rescue." He cocked an eye at sir Jeffrey.

"Done with the bloomin' thing yet, mate?"

"Done? Gads, man. This is a lifetime of work here. It has to be right or we might as well give up. Another half hour and I should be done with it."

"About time. You file it with the judge tomorrow?"

"Maybe, maybe. I want it to be perfect."

Painstakingly he traced in the last of the border work. He leaned back and inspected it. Yes, good. The printing had been done somewhere in Missouri with old English block letters and looked absolutely genuine. It only had to go back to the year 1845, not even thirty years ago.

He compared his work with an engraving in a book, and smiled. Yes. It might not fool the experts in the Tower of London, but out here in the backside of America, it would take months, perhaps years to disprove this certificate.

"Edward, see you're lifting the level of your reading. Up to the trashy dime novels, I see. Good lad. When we come into our fortune, you can buy some real books."

"Where would we keep them, guv'nor, in your carpetbag? We're not the type to carry too much luggage, especially when we're running to catch a stage or a train."

"Once you have money, dingo, nobody cares where it came from. Just having it is what's important. You'll see. We'll go back to New York and set up a flat and be the rage of the town's social season. We can do that with money. Especially here in the colonies."

Sir Jeffrey filled in the missing date by hand, since that was how the rest of the certificates had been drawn. There was little left to do. He would keep the finished document in the sun in the morning to help yellow it just a bit and to heat in the new ink and give it a touch of age. Not too much, it was supposed to be only thirty years old. The parchment paper he had used would be almost impossible to assign a date to, no matter how hard they tried.

His ink was of the oldest variety he could find in London. This was an operation that had been planned well in advance. And within a week at the most, the juicy plums would start falling into their grasp!

He pushed the parchment aside, carefully put away the two books and the letters and samples, and then stared down at the parchment with satisfaction. It was going to work! They had a shot at becoming millionaires! A million dollars, American. Two hundred thousand pounds sterling! The sum was staggering.

He put everything away, locked the cases and made sure the parchment lay between clean pillowcases to prevent any damage. Tomorrow he would give it the sun treatment, then perhaps present it. The Circuit Court judge would not be in La Grande much longer.

Edward checked his pocket watch, put away his novel and straightened up the room. Sir Jeffrey hardly noticed. When the knock came on the door, Sir Jeffrey scowled.

"Not again, you didn't invite that whore here again tonight!" Sir Jeffrey whined.

"No," Edward said, grinning. He swung open the door. "I invited two fresh ones, one for you, one for me. No, no, old friend, don't thank me. Just take your pick, and hurry into your room with her. These two are both hot and we don't want them to cool down."

The two saloon girls rushed into the room, spun around, and then began undressing. Sir Jeffrey cowered against a chair.

"Edward! You know perfectly well that I don't care for this sort of thing."

"He's shy, ladies. Takes a bit of warming up." Edward pulled Sir Jeffrey to the side of the room. "The taller one is yours. She's not a big titted whore. Brought her for you. She's got such small tits you'll think she's a boy. Roll her over on her belly and have at her hard little ass. You'll think she's a sixteen year old lad, you will. Now have a go at her. If that don't work she's got a well trained mouth, I can vouch for that. You can do a little putting instead of taking, old man!"

By this time both girls were naked, prancing around the middle of the room. Edward grabbed the one with breasts and vanished into one of the bedrooms.

The tall, thin girl came up to Sir Jeffrey and rubbed his crotch. Then she knelt in front of him and had his fly open before he knew what was happening. Sir Jeffrey closed his eyes as she stripped him and led him into the other bedroom.

Edward had been right. With his eyes closed she did feel like a ripe young sixteen year old male ruffian from London. It might not be such a wasted night after all.

It was nearly eight-thirty that evening when someone knocked hard on the Presidential suite door. Neither Sir Jeffrey nor Edward wanted to answer it. After eight knockings, with each one becoming more insistent, Edward pulled on his britches and went to the door.

A tall, thin man with a three day stubble of beard pushed into the room. His hands hung at the end of long arms like afterthoughts. His eyes roamed the room, then stopped at Edward.

"Where's the rest of my money?" the man said, his voice a rasping, unhealthy sound.

"Digger, you fucking idiot! You got your money. Why are you bothering us?"

The hands shot upward, caught around Edward's throat and squeezed suddenly and hard. At once Edward's eyes bulged, he couldn't breathe and began wheezing and gasping. His arms flailed at the man. One fist hit the tall man's eye and he let go of Edward and turned away to the side.

They stared at each other. Edward at last got his breath back and the tall man held one hand over his wounded eye.

"My money," the man Edward called Digger snarled. "You still owe me fifty dollars."

"Maybe so. Let me talk to my partner." Edward pulled open Sir Jeffrey's door. He was just coming away from the woman who lay on the bed on her stomach.

"Thought you'd like that," Edward said with a knowing grin. Then he frowned. "There's a bloke out here who claims we still owe him fifty dollars. Didn't you pay Digger the whole thing three weeks ago?"

Sir Jeffrey shook his head. "We were short, remember? He's here? Pay him and get him on his way to Portland. Do it right now!"

"I thought he was out of the state by now," Edward said. "Damn! Got to do every bloody thing myself." He went out banging the door. Sir Jeffrey shrugged and crawled back on the bed.

"Now show me that trick you have of getting me ready to go again fast!"

In the next room, Edward dug into his poke and

came up with two double eagles and a gold eagle and gave them to the tall, thin man.

"I want you on the first stage out of here in the morning, do you understand?" Edward said.

Digger stared at the money and ignored him.

Edward grabbed a knife from his pocket, snapped open the blade and pressed it against the tall man's throat.

"Mate, I'll tell you once more, then I'll save me fifty dollars. You be on that stage coach for Portland in the morning the way we agreed, right?"

Slowly the man's anger faded enough so he could nod. He grunted an assent.

"Now get your bloody arse out of here, and use the back stairs. If I see you anywhere near this hotel or us again, I'll slice your throat from ear to ear, mate. You understand what I'm telling you?"

"Yes. I waited for the money. Your fault, not mine." The man glared at Edward, turned and went out the door. He continued down the back stairs, anxious not to be seen by the hotel people. They had thrown him out several times. He did not like any of them.

Nobody ever liked him. Wasn't his fault. They were afraid of him. Not very many, he hadn't hurt very many of them. When he did they stayed hurt. He laughed, remembering the fire. Now that had been fun! He liked to watch things burn.

Just because people called him Digger wasn't his fault, either. So he dug the graves out at the cemetery. Somebody had to do it. They paid him a dollar for every one, digging and filling in. He even had a little house out in back of the graveyard. Just one room and he made it himself. He didn't have to pay rent.

Damn, that fire had been fun! He wasn't sure
what the other two guys were doing, but he had
sure as shit burned down that fucking house in
good order! Yeah! He thought about it and
remembered how it was, and soon he was
breathing faster and faster. He realized he was
getting all heated up. Damn prick stood straight
up inside his pants! A fire, yeah, he *needed*
another goddamned fucking it to hell fire!

Digger ran now, straight back to his shack
behind the graves. He took out the two one-gallon
cans of kerosene, the kind everybody had for their
lamps. He shook them. Both were full. Yeah, he
had filled them just yesterday down at the hardware store. They had a big barrel out on the back
dock.

Digger grinned as he lifted the cans. One might
do it, this time. No, he wouldn't be inside, he
better take two. He felt along the inside of the
shack up high where he kept the matches. He
didn't want no mouse to bite into a match and
burn down his shack!

The tall, gaunt man with dirt from today's
grave still on his pants, carried the two gallons of
coal oil as he walked down one alley after another
trying to pick a good house to burn down. He
wanted just a house, not the whole town. Lordy,
he couldn't stand it if more than one place burned
at a time! Both his hand and his prick would just
wear out!

Digger laughed. It had been two or three weeks
since he'd laughed.

The big house on the corner looked like a good
one. All wood and white paint, two stories tall,
and already the lights were out in the big house.
He had no idea who lived there. It would make a

beautiful fire, and everyone could see from all around. He walked past it, then went into the alley behind it and melted into a shadow.

Digger was good at waiting. He had to do a lot of waiting in his business. He had learned to be patient. An hour after he got there he saw someone come home to the big house. Lights flared, and burned for two more hours. Then, about midnight the last lamp was blown out on the second floor.

He gave them another half hour to get to sleep, then moved cautiously through shadows to the side of the house. One window had not been locked. He lifted it silently, cautiously and looked inside. A sitting room. Curtains. He reached inside and splashed half the gallon of coal oil and let it soak into the rug and furniture.

Then he went to the other side of the house. The window he wanted was locked. He took off his shirt and held it against the glass, then broke it with one sharp, powerful blow from the side of his fist. The glass broke, but the sound had been deadened by the cloth. Quickly he dumped the rest of the first gallon of kerosene inside, then put his shirt back on. He went to the back porch. Porches were always good. He tried the screen door. It was held by a hook and eye. With his knife he slit the screen wire and lifted the hook free. The door swung open.

Inside the back porch, he poured out two quarts of the kerosene, then left the can half filled beside the wall. Now he lit the fuel, and tore up some newspapers to help it burn.

Digger ran to each side of the house, firing the evaporating coal oil with burning newspapers. Then he walked away rapidly. He was a block away when he saw flames behind him. They shot out a window on the side of the house.

Someone screamed. He sat down on a small lawn a block away and watched. It was past midnight.

Digger heard more screams coming from down the block. Then men appeared from houses. They were wearing trousers, pajamas and slippers. Each man carried two or more buckets and ran quickly toward the fire.

The tall, thin man with the sunken eyes and nervous, claw like hands walked that way. Five minutes later he was in a line running buckets of water to the house. There was no chance to save it.

After half an hour the whole upper floor was burning. One man had jumped from the second floor. He had a broken leg.

"My wife's still up there!" he screamed again and again. Two men held him down so he wouldn't try to hobble back into the fire to find his wife.

Digger sat on the lawn across the street with a dozen or so other men from the bucket brigade. All were soaked and sweating; smoke clouded their eyes and black smudges showed on their clothes.

"Hell, we tried," one man said.

Digger nodded. "Damn right, we tried."

9

From the county jail, Spur went back to the Sagebrush Saloon to check on the girl, be sure she was all right, and he wanted to hear her sing again. He enjoyed it. There wasn't a lot of entertainment on the range out here. Half the men evidently in town felt the same way.

The Sagebrush was packed when he walked in the front door. Men sat on the stairs, stood shoulder to shoulder in front of the stage and those at the tables in back had to stand up to see when Colette came out and played her fanfare on the old piano.

Everyone in the bar went as silent as a silver moon on a clear lake.

"Good evening, gentlemen. I'm glad that you came to hear me sing. Don't be bashful about buying your favorite refreshment while you're here. I also invite you to feed the kitty on the bar if you like my singing. Just between you and me, I don't share that kitty with Lefty who owns this place." The audience laughed and the kitty began making the rounds.

Colette romped into a dozen songs, mostly old favorites the men knew, as well as a few Civil War songs and a new tune or two that none of them had heard before.

The half hour of singing and piano playing was over too quickly and the men coaxed another five minutes of song from her. Twice she had caught Spur's eye while she sang. He had been standing at the back beside the bar.

Lefty came down the bar, wiped the spot in front of Spur and set out a cold bottle of beer.

"Courtesy of Colette," he said softly. "She says if you have a minute she would like to talk to you in her dressing room after the show. Usually I don't let anybody in there, but with you I guess it will be all right."

Spur took the cold beer with him and went through a small door at the side of the bar. It opened on a short hall with two doors. One was open and he saw Colette sitting in front of a mirror inside. When she saw him she stood and smiled.

"I want to thank you for saving my skin tonight. Nobody has had the nerve to handle John Ringo the way you did. He was going to rape me, you know."

"Yes, it occurred to me."

"My last show is a ten-thirty. I hope you can be here. I want you to walk me back to my hotel. I don't like being out late at night and alone. It's only two blocks, but . . ."

"I'll be here. Looks like you'll have a job here at the Sagebrush for quite a while. The men love hearing you sing and play."

"Good. Only then I'll have to get some new

dresses. I can't show up on stage every night in the same old clothes."

"Tough problem," Spur said grinning.

"Nice kind of problem to have." She walked near him and put one hand behind Spur's neck and pulled his face down to meet hers.She stood on tiptoe and kissed his lips softy, then let him go.

"That's a first thank you. Now I usually try to have a small nap between shows. Idea! here's twenty dollars. Play poker with it for me and see if I win anything. That will give you something to do between shows."

"Fair enough. Maybe we'll get lucky tonight."

She smiled. I hope so."

Back in the saloon and gaming house, the crowd had thinned out to a normal number, and Spur found an empty chair at a small stakes poker game. No bet over a dollar. He sat down, got change and concentrated on his poker.

He used only her double eagle as his stake, and before the last show was announced at ten-thirty, he had almost fifty dollars on the table in front of him. The game broke up and he took Colette's winnings and moved closer to the stage.

It was a great performance, with half the songs new. Colette seemed to know almost every popular song that the men requested during that part of her show.

Again the bar was filled shoulder to shoulder, and the extra barkeep was kept busy selling drinks along with Lefty. When the show was over most of the patrons finished their drinks and left. It was eleven o'clock, late for a farming, ranch oriented kind of people who lived in La Grande.

Spur sat at the end of the bar near the small

door and waited. Ten minutes after the show ended, Colette came out wearing the same dress. She now sported a small hat over her long black hair.

"Ready for your guard duty?" she asked smiling.

"Anytime you are."

She said good night to Lefty, told him she would be back at eight-thirty the next evening and they went out the door. She put her hand out holding his bent arm, and looked up at him.

"I really appreciate this. I still get the shivers remembering how easily John Ringo picked me up. I was paralyzed."

"Think about something else, like the twenty dollars that grew into fifty for you tonight. You won thirty dollars!"

"That's a whole month's wages! I should stake you every night." She shook her head. "No, I can't do that. I'm still upset about John Ringo."

"Think about something else."

"Home. I usually think about home. I guess I miss the storms most, those fierce storms that sweep in from the Atlantic in winter, smashing things, battering the cliffs, changing the coastline. It generates an excitement in the whole town. You never know if you're going to be washed away or blown away."

"Sounds like a place I'll stay away from."

"You would love it. Don't you like a noisy thunder and lightning storm? All that power, that force, and puny little man is down here looking up and hoping a lightning bolt doesn't hit his house or barn."

"I admit I enjoy a good lightning display."

"I'm here at the Grande Ronde Hotel, she said.

Second floor."

"That's a popular floor. What room?"

"Two oh one."

"The first one by the stairs. In case of fire—a quick escape."

Colette nodded. "Most people never think of that." She fished in her small reticule for her room key, unlocked the door and stepped inside. "Come in for a minute. I have a new bottle of what is supposed to be really good wine. You must sample it with me."

The room was a copy of his, looking out on Main Street. She took off the small hat and found the bottle of wine in a suitcase under the bed. She magically produced two glasses.

"I stole the glasses from the saloon."

The wine was corked and she found a corkscrew and let Spur do the honors opening the bottle. He screwed the metal into the cork as far as he thought he dared, then holding the bottle pulled slowly on the cork. It came out with a resounding pop, and for a moment he wondered if it were champagne.

"No, just a good red wine," she told him.

She poured.

The wine was surprisingly good.

"It's from California," she said. "I think they have at last learned how to make wine down there."

She put the glass down and sat on the bed and motioned for him to sit beside her.

"Spur, I have a favor to ask. I don't do this very often, but tonight is special, and I think you are a special man. I want you to softly, and gently, make love to me." She watched him for a moment, then bent forward and kissed his lips, easily at first, then with more and more desire.

When the kiss was done she smiled. "You don't seem surprised."

"Very little a beautiful woman ever does surprises me. I'm pleased, flattered, interested, anxious. But not surprised."

He bent forward this time and kissed her lips, then both her eyes and then the side of her throat.

Her voice was very soft and low. "Spur, you will have to seduce me. I may even protest a little."

"But you are sure?"

"Oh, yes! I want to be with you, right here, right now."

He kissed her again, then put his arms around her.

"Now, tell me about Portland, your home. Tell me all about your family and how you learned to sing, and where you memorized all of the songs."

She began talking, and as she did Spur kissed her and held her and now and then stroked her breasts throug the fabric. She looked at him quickly at first, then smiled. It took him ten minutes of talking and stroking before she let him keep his hand over her breast. The soft massaging led to her gasping with pleasure and a smile now and then.

It took him a half hour to get the front of her dress unbuttoned, and another half hour before he could slip his hand under her chemise and hold her bare breast.

Slowly he pushed the dress off her shoulders and let it fall around her waist. Then little by little he lifted her chemise away so her breasts were uncovered.

He kissed them and she whimpered with excitement. At last he found the combination to the dress and lifted it over her head. The three petticoats went down off her feet and she lay on the bed, topless, her face a combination of surprise and wonder.

Twice he had moved her hands to his crotch, but she would not open his fly. At last he did so himself and pushed her hands inside. Cautiously, slowly they explored until they found his erection.

She moaned with delight.

He stripped his clothes off, locked the door and pushed a chair under the handle, then sat on the bed beside her. She reached out and touched his erection, then grasped it and watched him.

His hands touched the drawers she wore, cotton underpants that extended down each leg to the knee.

"Sweet Colette, I think it's time we take these off, don't you?" She nodded, but her hands held his hands.

"Maybe we should just get dressed again," she said.

Spur sat up. "Fine. You want to get dressed, fine with me. Then I can get to my room and get some sleep."

"No! I want to do it, I really do. Help me, please."

"Give me your hands."

She did. He put both of them around his erection.

"Now, don't move your hands, all right?"

Colette shivered, but nodded.

Spur unbuttoned the drawers, and slowly took them off, pulling them down her legs.

Colette whimpered softly. He kissed her. He

caught her hands and put them round his neck, then he kissed her and slowly, gently he rolled over on top her.

Colette trembled and her whole body went stiff. For a moment she didn't breathe.

"It's all right, Colette. Everything is fine. This is normal and natural." He kissed her then and she relaxed and opened her eyes.

"Am I being terrible?"

"No, just frightened. I can't figure out why. Have you ever made love before?"

"Not soft and gentle, not this way."

"Oh, It should always be this way." He bent and kissed her breasts, licking her nipples until he saw them lift and enlarge.

"Does that feel good, warm and nice?"

"Yes."

"That's how making love feels."

When his hand at last moved down to her crotch, she was soft and wet. Slowly, gently, he edged against her and then inside. She moaned and smiled and then grabbed his buttocks and pushed him in harder until his long shaft was all the way home.

Colette sighed.

"I think I like this," she said softly.

Spur found her hard clit and twanged it four times. She gasped and yelped and then surged into a shattering, stunning climax that kept her vibrating and throbbing for over sixty seconds. When the tremors passed sweat streaked her forehead and her face.

"That, that . . . that was so *wonderful*! That has never happened before. Never! So fine, so marvelous." She was beaming. Colette looked up and kissed his lips. "Now nice man, Spur McCoy, who has been so patient with me. It's your turn."

Spur had been holding back for the past forty-five minutes. Now he stroked a dozen times and exploded with a punching series of thrusts, then he settled beside her on the bed.

"You are fantastic in bed," Spur said.

Colette laughed softly and stroked his chest. "You are the one who helped me to find that out. The next time will be a little easier. But I think I always will remember too much about before."

Spur frowned. "What about before? Can you tell me about it?"

She shook her head. "No, that is for forgetting. I never will be able to talk about it. Just thinking is bad enough." She picked up his hand and moved it to her crotch.

"Make me feel so wonderful again, wonderful Spur McCoy."

His finger found the spot and this time she sailed for twice as long over the moon and the stars and saw the wonder of the universe. When at last she settled beside him again, she thanked him and slowly drifted off to sleep.

Spur lifted away from her, slid into his clothes, and closed the door so the chair would slide under the door knob. Back in his room he found that nothing had been disturbed, no one had been there. He locked the door and window, then dropped into bed.

When the fire burned down the mayor's big house that night, just after midnight, all of the commotion and shouting and screams two blocks away did not even wake up Spur McCoy.

10

Spur heard about the fire the next morning at breakfast. As soon as he was through, he went to the burned house and looked at it. The sheriff had been there and left. Near where the back porch had been, Spur found a tin can, the kind kerosene usually came in.

Another similar can that had burned almost to the point of melting, still sat beside the back wall of the house inside the old porch. The rest of the house had burned completely. Only part of the heavy staircase had not gone up in smoke.

Spur took the can that had only been scorched by the fire. There was still some printing on the side of the rectangular can. Who would sell kerosene? He checked at two stores before he found one, the hardware dealer.

The man was in his sixties, loved the hardware business and said he was a problem solver.

"What's your problem, young man?"

Spur held up the can. "This come from your store?"

The hardware man took it and turned it around, read the printing left on the metal and nodded.

"Right you are, but I can't say when. Sell a few of these fresh, but most folks bring them back for a refill from my big barrel out in back. Less expensive that way."

"You fill any yesterday?"

"Half a dozen. Seems like we do about that many a day winter or summer. Course, now, in the winter lots of folks have those little coal oil heaters, the round kind that don't need a chimney. Makes the house smell a little, but it's a quick way to get some more heat in a place. We sell lots more kerosene then, usually in five gallon cans."

"Remember who got refills last couple of days?"

"Not off hand. I could think on it."

"Good, I'm working with the sheriff. We just might have a fire starter in town. The mayor's house was torched using coal oil from that can. You might help us find out who it was."

"Well now, don't that beat all! A fire starter! I'll work up a list for you right off."

Spur thanked him and walked over to the county sheriff's office and jail. He heard John Ringo swearing as soon as he came in the front door.

Sheriff Younger shook his head. "You got to get that guy out of here, McCoy. You said you'd talk to him, you'd take responsibility. So do it!"

Spur went back to the cell. John Ringo shook the bars and glared at Spur.

"Calm down Ringo, or you'll never see daylight again. You could be in big trouble. No self defense involved in this."

"In what, damnit? You hit me."

"You were committing assault and battery on a female. You were threatening to rape her. Oregon courts could give you five years in prison for that. They protect their womenfolk out here."

Ringo calmed down. "But I was drunk. I don't rape women. All women are special. I must have got some bad whiskey."

"You were roaring drunk, I brought you in. Now, you want to get out of here without a trial?"

"Yeah."

"First you agree to be on the one o'clock stage for Portland. Give me your word."

"Hell . . . okay. My job here is done. I'll be on the damn stagecoach."

"Good. Next I want you to promise not to hurt the sheriff or any of his deputies. They were just doing their job. Give me your word on that."

Ringo looked at the sheriff who came to the side of the cell.

"Right, all right. I won't gun down any of the sheriff's people here. Now you have my word."

Sheriff Younger still looked scared. He frowned at Spur and motioned him to one side.

"You going to take the word of a killer like Ringo? That won't mean a damn thing to him."

"With Ringo, it does. I've heard that he is scrupulously honest about standing behind his word. I'm betting on it. If not, I'll be around. Get the keys."

Sheriff Younger shook his head, hesitated, then at last gave the key to the cell to Spur. McCoy unlocked the cell door.

"Pick up whatever you had in your pockets at the desk," Spur said.

Ringo snorted and went through the door to the

front of the office where Sheriff Younger was taking items from a drawer.

"A hundred and ten dollar and twenty seven cents, a knife, two small rocks and a harmonica."

Ringo nodded. "Sounds about right. Now my two six-guns."

"You a man of your word, Ringo?"

"Damn right. Give me my guns."

Sheriff Younger handed the gun belt and the two Colts to Younger who strapped them on. He turned and looked at Spur who leaned against the wall.

John Ringo stared at Spur with a deadly gleam in his eyes.

"Yeah, now I remember. Spur McCoy, big time Federal lawman. Heard about you in Arizona. I made my promises not to hurt the sheriff, but that didn't include you, McCoy. I want your hide!"

"Could be trouble for you, Ringo."

"And could be dead for you, McCoy."

"Let's have a real Texas walk-down. One shot each. Whoever shoots first has to stand pat after he fires. If he hits the other man, fine. If he misses or just wounds him, the one who hasn't fired yet can walk down the line and blast the other one from two feet if he wants to. A Texas Walk-down shootout."

"Not a chance, Ringo. I'll take you on the regular way. Five rounds in one gun and fifty yards apart. Then we walk forward."

"Fifty yards? No damn six-gun is good at that range. Fifty feet maybe if you're lucky."

Spur drew the special Colt from his holster. It had a ten inch barrel on it.

"It's not fast draw, Ringo, but it's damn

accurate at forty yards. You still want to call me out?''

"Damn right! You probably can't even hold that thing steady. Since I have to be on the one o'clock stage, let's make our showdown at high noon on Main Street. Right outside of the doctor's office so he can pronounce you dead.''

Spur grinned. "Suits me. The sheriff will have a couple of men there with shotguns to insure a fair fight.'' Spur turned and walked away. He had never liked call-outs, and avoided these duel-like shootouts whenever he could. But this one was not to be denied. Ringo's pride had been injured, and he would not stop until he had a chance to repair the damage. Killing Spur would suit him just fine.

Until noon, Spur had work to do. He headed back toward the hardware store hoping the owner would have that list. Whoever torched the house was hired by someone, or was the brains behind this whole land grab. It could be a good lead. There was no reason the person who used kerosene had bought it during the last two days, but it was a chance. Right now Spur would take any kind of help he could find.

He passed the courtroom where the circuit judge was in his last day of hearings before he moved to the next town. Someone came running out of the building, his face ashen, fear crowding in on his stern features.

"My god! it can't be! It just can't be true! Twenty years of hard work for nothing?''

Spur stopped the man. "What's going on?''

"Courthouse. Some Englishman claims he has a British Crown Land Grant that covers almost all of Wallowa county. He says he owns the whole

damn county, the town the hills, everything. He
claims everyone here is a trespasser on his land!''

Land again. Land! It could tie in with the land
records burning! Spur ran for the court and
squeezed into the packed room. Sir Jeffrey
Mountbatten was standing near the judge
talking.

"Your Honor, I don't know how to make it any
plainer. This document has recently come into my
hand. The Royal land grant was made in 1845 to
my father the late Earl of Mountbatten to reward
him for long service to the queen. I am his only
heir and now own the land grant. Queen Victoria
made hundreds of land grants.

"As I'm sure you know the Oregon territory
was jointly occupied by the United States and the
British Empire by agreement in 1818 and
renewed in 1827. The boundaries were finalized in
1846 when the 49th parallel was established as
the international boundary between the British
Canada and the U.S. The boundary extended
from the Pacific Ocean to the Rocky Mountains.

"There seems little to dispute. Her Royal
Majesty, Queen Victoria, had the absolute right
to award a Royal Land Grant in this territory.
Simply because the document was lost or not
claimed for the past thirty years, has no bearing
on its authenticity.

"I'm sure you have numerous ways to check
the form and content of such a document. And
when you do I am certain that you will find it
authentic in every way. Even though I own this
vast area of land, I realize that I now am under
the authority and legal jurisdiction of the United
States Government, and your court.

"That is why I have brought the document to

your attention just as soon as I received it by post and messenger from London. I have been in town for almost a month waiting for it to arrive. I'm sure you understand the delays that occur on ocean as well as land transport."

Judge Farley Inglesia stared at the paper in his hands. It was a fine parchment, and the royal crest and printing all looked accurate. He read the description of the area again and was thunderstruck.

". . . that the grant shall include all of those areas drained by rivers said to be named the Grande Ronde, the Joseph and the Innaha from their sources to their joining the Snake river."

"Mr. Mountbatten. The court would have appreciated some kind of advance notice of a land claim of this magnitude. Nothing of this sort has ever taken place in Oregon before. In fact I can think of no British Royal Land grant ever having the support of law anywhere in the Western part of the nation.

"Numerous Spanish Land Grants have been ruled valid in California, but those were entirely different circumstances. There the owners had been long time residents and toilers on the land they claimed."

"Your Honor, I understand the shock of this revelation. I, too, was surprised by the extent of the claim. I have been touring my land lately and it indeed is extensive. However, I am more than willing to wait for the decision of this court in the matter. I am a law abiding, peaceful man, and I urge everyone in the county to have patience."

"Mr. Mountbatten," the Judge said. "There is no possibility that the court can rule on this document today. Indeed it would be my first opinion that it would have to be taken up with the Federal District court in Portland. However this court will retain the document which has been properly marked and recorded by the clerk.

"Knowing the gravity of this claim, the court will seek all possible haste and forward the document to Portland on the stage which I understand leaves this noon. It will be sent by an armed and bonded messenger to insure its safety. A copy of the wording and descriptions will be made by the clerk and made available here through the county offices."

"Your Honor, do you have any estimate about the length of time the Federal court might take . . ."

"None whatsoever, Mr. Mountbatten. However, I urge the people of the county not to jump to conclusions. Since this type of land grant has never been presented before, we can not know how the court will rule. It could rule it invalid under international law. Or it could rule it valid. We'll just have to wait for the decision of the court."

"Thank you your honor." Sir Jeffrey Mountbatten closed a small leather case he carried, nodded to his man, Edward Long, and they made their way out of the small, packed court room. Spur moved out behind them.

Once on the street a man who had followed them out charged Sir Jeffrey and knocked him down.

"If I had a gun I'd kill you!" he screamed. "My whole life's savings are tied up in my land and my house. I'll never let you have them." He kicked at Sir Jeffrey and Edward Long jumped to his aid.

Spur's long pistol came out and he fired one

shot in the air.

"Stop it! That's enough! The matter is up to the court."

A dozen more men stormed from the court chambers and headed for Sir Jeffrey. Spur saw that it was quickly developing into a riot he could not control. He grabbed the Englishman and raced him down the alley, then along another block until they came to the livery.

"You would have been ripped to pieces back there in another five minutes," Spur said. "You should have expected some violent sort of reaction to a bombshell like this."

"Really I had no thought that there would be any violence. It's a matter for the law."

They panted for a moment.

"You don't threaten two or three thousand people with the total loss of their land and houses and businesses and their whole future without expecting some reaction. Now we better get you out of town before you two go to a necktie party with a real hemp rope."

11

Spur quickly rented three horses with saddles
and they rode down the alley, across three back
yards and around a small farm. Then they were in
the open range and Spur angled toward the river
and a grove of trees which was about three miles
from the main part of town.

"I don't believe it," Sir Jeffrey said. "We are
actually running for our lives. How droll."

"If you don't want to be shot down, or get your
neck stretched by a rope, you better concentrate
on riding, and forget the try at being funny,"
Spur said.

Spur watched behind but could see no
immediate pursuit. That didn't mean someone
would not raise a gang, a small mob and come
charging after them later.

"We can't just stay out here in the wilderness,"
Sir Jeffrey said.

"Oh, for bloody hell . . .!" Edward Long burst
out suddenly, glaring at Sir Jeffrey. Then he
stopped quickly.

Spur eased the pace down to a walk. They were almost to the woods.

"All you have to do is wait out here and hide if anybody comes looking for you. As soon as it gets dark, ride back into town and I'll meet you in back of the hotel. I'll have rented a room for you. Don't go back to your regular rooms wherever they are. You can bet somebody with a loaded shotgun has already visited them."

"These people mean business, don't they?" Sir Jeffrey said, more serious than he had been before.

"You threaten their whole way of life in this county and reduce everyone living here to a pauper. That is bound to come as a shock. I don't see how any court can accept the authenticity of your Royal Land Grant. It would mean chaos in the county, and upset things in this half of the state."

"I can't argue that point with you. But the land really belongs to me, to my family . . "

"We'll let the court decide. But none of that will matter to you a bit if you're dead and buried. So keep a sharp lookout. You have a watch?"

"Yes, of course."

"I'll meet you in back of the Grande Ronde Hotel at eight o'clock. It will be dark then. Don't let anyone recognize you as you ride into La Grande.

Spur turned his horse and rode away. He circled the little town and came in from the opposite direction.

Back in the three block long business section, the whole of La Grande was in an uproar. Everywhere on the street groups of men were talking. Some were urging that they raise a posse and go hunt down the Englisher. Others said such a claim would never hold up in court. No Royal Land Grant like this had ever been sanctioned by the courts in Oregon before.

A few wondered if the claim was real or not. They wondered how a judge in Oregon would be able to rule on a document that might or might not have been signed by Queen Victoria in London.

Spur worked his way through the people to the little hospital wing. On the way he had stopped at the La Grande General Mercantile and bought a box of chocolates.

He gave them to Rebecca Jonas. She now had both eyes uncovered. Neither was damaged, but her right cheek was still bandaged.

"Nobody done brought me chocolates in ten years," she said. "Jonas was a good man, but not a romantic." She offered Spur one of the delicacies but he declined.

"Have you remembered anything else about the night of the fire?"

"Yes, I have, Mr. McCoy, and I think it could be important. The key word is duplicate. I remember Jonas saying part of the extra work he had was because the former clerk kept all of his records in duplicate. He made two entries on two sets of permanent record books. The old man was terrified of fire.

"So when Jonas took over, the old man made him promise to keep up all of the duplicate records."

"Duplicate. If the former clerk was so worried about fire, he must have kept one set of the records in another place. Did Jonas ever say anything about having to take things to another building, or did he work at the city owned building?"

"He never said anything like that. I just know he was doing two or three men's jobs. He worked twelve to thirteen hours every day, except the Lord's day, of course."

"Did the land office ever have a safe?"

"No, we didn't handle money. Oh, for the records? Land sakes no. Those big books are almost three feet square. Take a whole vault to hold them."

"Vault, the bank. Let me go give Mr. Follette a call. That might solve a lot of our problems." Spur smiled down at the woman. "Now, Rebecca, you just eat those chocolates and hurry up and get well. I'll see you again."

Five minutes later Hirum Follette shook his head. They had just probed and moved things and looked in every square inch of the bank's new vault. It was made of six inches of steel and concrete, and was absolutely fireproof. But there were no county land records inside.

"Sorry, McCoy. I really hoped that those ledgers had been brought over here. Guess not."

Spur thanked him and left. There were fewer people on the streets now, but everywhere the topic of conversation was the Queen Victoria Land Grant. As the shock of it wore off, more and more people were downplaying it. Something like this could take years to resolve going through the courts.

More and more people wondered if the Land Grant was really from Queen Victoria. Spur had thought of the chance that the paper was a complete fake. His half hour with the two Englishmen did nothing to dispel that possibility. If it was a phony, the courts would discover it quickly, but that wouldn't help Spur find out who had killed Jonas King, or where the duplicate land records were.

He went to the burned out land office. It was just the way it had been. He found a solid two-by-four and began probing the ground. The building had been pier-block and joyce built, and all the flooring and most of the supporting joyce had burned away. He walked through the blackened jungle, probing with the two by four, stabbing the ground, looking for a cave, a hole, even the hard surface of a big floor vault where the records might have been kept.

Jonas and Rebecca had moved into the old home which had been taken over by the count to house the county clerk's office. So the former clerk could have had a little cellar dug. But after two hours of probing and falling down and ruining a good shirt with the charcoal and ashes, Spur decided there was no hidden area under the house.

What next?

He sat on the small swatch of grass in the front yard. The only other chance was the small stable house where one horse could be kept. Spur was about to move in that direction when he checked his watch. It was five minutes until noon. He had a date with John Ringo.

Spur had no desire to shoot it out with Ringo close-up. But with his long barreled pistol he had an even chance. That was better odds than he usually enjoyed.

Three or four years ago, Spur had gone to the longer weapon. He found it shot much straighter and more accurately, and that he could hit what he aimed for at ranges well over a hundred feet.

Most six-guns with their seven and a half inch barrels were notoriously inaccurate. His only hope now was to aim straight and shoot first.

Word of the gunfight had spread almost as fast as that about the Land Grant. Fifty people had come out of stores and stood on the boardwalks watching.

At the far end of the long block in front of the Sagebrush Saloon, stood John Ringo. He held a fifth of whiskey in his left hand and from time to time took a drink.

Spur McCoy came out of the side street and stood at the other end of the block. He adjusted the long weapon in his holster and waited.

"You wanted a long walk, you got it," Ringo called.

"You have one last chance to get on the stage without a bullet in you, Ringo." Spur answered.

"Not a chance," Ringo said and turned, showing that he only had one gun. He corked the whiskey bottle and tossed it to a man on the boardwalk. "Save that for me, I'll want it again in about two minutes."

"Let's do it, Ringo," Spur called. They stared at each other and then began walking forward. They were about fifty yards apart. No one was behind either man, but the boardwalks were filled. More people ran in to watch.

Spur drew his long weapon after five full strides. He stopped, spread his feet apart and lifted the weapon.

"Look at the barrel on that Colt!" somebody called.

Spur brought the gun up to shoulder height and reached out with his left hand, using both arms and hands to steady the weapon. He sighted in on Ringo's right shoulder, blinked as Ringo took another step. He would fire just before the next step by Ringo's right foot. The gunfighter's weapon was still in leather. They were thirty-eight yards apart.

Spur held his breath, refined the sight again on the shoulder and squeezed off the shot.

The blast of the .44 round came like a thunder-clap, only to be topped by the shouts of surprise and amazement as John Ringo took the round in his left shoulder and sprawled backwards in the dust of the unpaved street.

He glared at Spur, but his right arm hung use-less. His own six-gun had spilled from leather and lay three feet away. Ringo grabbed at it with his left hand, but already Spur had sighted in and fired. The chunk of .44 caliber lead it the cylinder of the Colt .44 and slammed it a dozen feet back-wards out of the reach of John Ringo.

Spur walked up and looked down at the famous gunfighter.

"Told you I had no cause to kill you, Ringo. You go see Doc George, and then you still have forty-five minutes to be on the stage. I'll keep that ruined .44 of yours."

Spur turned and walked away. John Ringo stared at Spur for a moment, then laughed.

"Damned if that long gun of his didn't beat me. Damned if it didn't! Learned something today." He looked around. "Who in hell has my bottle of whiskey? And where is that doctor's office? Somebody show me the way. I got a stagecoach to catch for Portland."

Spur kept walking to the building where the county held its court. Circuit Court Judge

Inglesia had canceled the rest of his afternoon calendar. His clerk said the judge would see Spur.

Spur had out his Federal identification when he walked into the judge's private, if temporary, chambers.

Judge Inglesia looked at the letter and nodded. "That's why you wanted to see me before. Now things are different. You know about the land grant claim?"

"Yes, Your Honor. I think it ties in with the land record fire. Nobody can prove who owns anything. Then the Royal Land Grant drops on the court and before you can blink, the Englishman owns everything."

"You're telling me you think the Englishman had something to do with burning up the land records?" The judge paused. "Yes, it would seem to follow. I have sent the document off to Portland. I really can't do anything else."

"I understand. I have a question. If that document turns out to be spurious, a forgery say, would it be a state or a federal crime? Who would have jurisdiction?"

"The Federal courts, no question. The Circuit Court is merely acting as a messenger service in this case."

Spur knew what he wanted. He thanked the judge, went back to his hotel and had his noontime meal, even if it was late. The rest of the afternoon he poked around the blackened ruins of the land office house, then checked with the hardware owner. He had four names of people who had bought more than one gallon of kerosene the previous three days in one gallon cans.

Two of them were women who lived alone. The third was the owner of the livery stable and the fourth the town's grave digger, a truly strange man known only as "Digger."

"Where does this Digger live," Spur asked.

"Where he works. He has a shack down in back of the graveyard. Spends most of his time down there when he isn't digging or filling in graves. A stranger man you'll never find, at least in this county."

Spur decided to pay the man a visit. The graveyard was at the end of town, closer to the big bend in the river. Spur walked, found the small shack at the far end of the unused section of the cemetery. No one was home. The Secret Service Agent leaned against a tree and waited for half an hour. Nobody came, so he went back to the hotel.

Digger had seen Spur coming through the cemetery. He was a stranger to Digger, and strangers usually meant trouble. Digger slipped into the brush along the edge of the Grande Ronde river and hunkered down, watching. The man called, knocked on the side of the wall, and then waited.

Digger had no idea why the man waited. When the stranger at last moved off through the cemetery, Digger remained hidden for a full hour before he left the trees and went back to the shack. He didn't want anything to do with strangers. Not a thing.

12

Well before eight o'clock that night, Spur had a
ground floor room rented only two doors down
from the side entrance of the Grande Ronde
Hotel. He explained that someone was trying to
find him he didn't want to see, so he wanted to
register the room under the name Mark Smith.
The clerk grinned thinking it was a love tryst.

Just after eight, the two men rode up on the
horses.

"McCoy? Is that you?" Sir Jeffrey whispered.

"Yes, leave the horses here. I'll take them back.
Now be quiet and we'll get into the room fast
before anyone can recognize you."

Spur took them into the room, told them to lock
the door and let him in when he got back from the
livery.

When Spur came back he brought a fifth of
whiskey and two kinds of wine.

"You men had anything to eat?" Spur asked.

"Hell no, and I'm hungry," Long said.

"We could do with some food," Sir Jeffrey said.

"I'll bring some plates from the dining room for my sick friends. Take a few minutes."

As Spur waited for the food to be fixed he realized how quickly the temper of the town had cooled off. Now less than ten hours after the first announcement of the Land Grant, La Grande had settled down and most people were willing to let the courts handle it. Many said no United States court was going to let some weird foreigner take their land away from them.

Spur brought the men dinners from the dining room, and then broke out the whiskey and soon both were feeling happy and talkative.

It was nearly two hours of drinking later before Spur got around to what he wanted to talk about with the two men.

"If you don't mind my asking, Sir Jeffrey, just why didn't your father come claim the land thirty years ago?"

"Oh, that's simple. He took sick and went to bed. He never told anyone about the grant, wanted to keep it as a surprise. Then a year later he died and only his solicitor knew of it. Father made him promise to wait to tell me about it until I was responsible. I was only a lad of six at the time, you see."

"Interesting," Spur said. "Here, let me freshen up that drink for you, we've got plenty for tonight. I'd guess that by tomorrow you'll be able to go back to your regular rooms. Tempers have cooled off a lot around town."

"Good. I'm tired of this small room already. Only one bed."

"Sir Jeffrey, how did your solicitor find you?"

"I wrote for money. I get a yearly stipend and it was due. He said now that I was thirty-five I was eligible for the Grant. Well, it was a shock and a surprise for me, I should tell you."

An hour later they were still drinking. Sir Jeffrey was showing signs of going to sleep. Spur had been sipping at his glass while pouring as much as he could for the Englishman.

When Sir Jeffrey passed out on the bed, Spur concentrated on Edward Long.

Spur laughed. "Now that old stuffed shirt there is blotto, we can talk, Edward. Is he really an Earl? I heard somewhere that he's a phony, making up all this Earl and Lord stuff to impress the ladies."

Long laughed. "Him impress the ladies? Not a chance. He'd rather pop you right now tonight, than the prettiest cunt you can find. He's bloody queer he is." Long took a good pull on the whiskey. "Things I could tell you about him. Gawd, you'd turn in your seat, you would."

"Is he a real Earl?"

"Nah . . . he lost his title cause he didn't go into the Queen's Service. Not really a Lord at all, but the Americans like to think he is. So we go along. Things I could bloody tell you about His Lordship, there. In Boston and then in New York. But loyalty is what I've got." He shook his head. "I must be drinking a little!" He laughed. Then had a long drink and blinked at Spur.

"Bloody stories I could tell. Good old Land Grant. Gonna be millionaires soon. Me I get fifty-fifty. Not that I did so much, but I'm part of the bloody team. Stories I could tell!"

"Edward, is the Land Grant Certificate really a forgery?" Spur asked.

Edward looked at him but never heard. He slumped sideways, then fell face down on the bed, passed out and began snoring in a moment.

Spur decided he had asked the most important question about a minute too late. He closed the door, locked it from the outside and slid the key under the door, then went up to his room. Long would be the better of the two for a little bit of Yankee informal questioning, but only after he recovered from tomorrow's hangover. The questioning would take place in what might be considered strange and wild circumstances. Spur smiled just thinking about it.

He unlocked his door and slipped inside. At once he smelled a perfume he remembered.

"Maggie Smith, you have returned," he said. He heard her giggle before he lit the lamp. He lit the wick, lowered the chimney and turned.

She sat on the bed wearing a soft cotton nightgown. Her brown eyes were alert and dancing. A smile creased her pretty face and she stretched.

"I've been waiting for you, hoping that you wouldn't be too late."

"Your daddy know you're in town?"

"Of course, I'm staying with my school chum. She always lies for me. I tell her when I'm in town. We are best friends, but she's already married."

"Did you come to stay the night?"

"Of course."

"You ran out early last time."

"I was worried that Daddy might come to town and stop by to see me. So I left here and rode back to the ranch."

As she said it she pulled the nightgown over her head. It barely fluttered her short cut blonde hair, but made her breasts jiggle from the motion.

"You make a pretty picture."

"I believe in going after what I want."

"What is that right now?"

"To have you come to bed with me and see how many times we can make love, a different way each time."

"You've had a lot of experience then, I would guess and know all about getting pregnant."

"No. I'm a ranch girl. I know all about breeding. I know when my fertile period is. Just after it's over, that's when I play married folks with you."

"Now."

"Yes."

"Do you mind if I lock the door and get undressed first?"

She giggled.

He locked the door, turning the key half way around so no one could get in with a pass key, then sat on the bed and pulled off his boots.

"I wish we had a bathtub here," she said. "I want to take a bath with you, but there's no chance." She moved up behind him and nibbled at his ear. Then she pushed her tongue into his ear, tickling him.

"Hurry!" she said.

She put her arms around him and unbuttoned his vest, then his shirt.

A moment later he was as bare as she was and slid under the one sheet she had left on the bed.

His arms went around her and she pressed hard against him.

"You have such a marvelous body! So strong and hard." She rolled over on top of him.

"Darling Spur, the first time this way! Oh, Please! Then you get to choose the next position.

I've never been done on top this way. It would be exciting!''

He pulled her head down and kissed her open mouth, then chewed and nibbled and sucked on her breasts hanging down at him like pointed, ripe mellons ready for picking.

"Do you know how it makes me feel when you're chewing on my titties? I get this warm, wonderful glow, like everything is wonderful and I'm pleased and happy. And then it grows and I get hotter and hotter, and if you lick my nipples I think they are going to burn right off! Did you know that? Lick my nipples again, darling Spur, oh please!''

She had found his pole and held it with one hand, stroking it back and forth gently. He licked her nipples and she groaned as a climax ripped into her slender form, rattling her like a tin cup in a bucket. She bounced and jolted and shivered. She let out a long, low wail and stopped pumping his penis.

Maggie gave one last shudder and relaxed on top of him, her breasts crushed against his chest, her chin just past his shoulder. She rested for two minutes, then pushed up and kissed him.

"Push it inside me quick before I scream!''

Maggie helped. Spur laughed as she rode him. She was panting and puffing and then she climaxed again just as he did and they roared and rumbled and came at the same time nearly knocking the springs out of the bedstead. At last they slowed and calmed and lay in each other's arms panting and gasping for breath.

A few minutes later she raised up from where she lay beside him. She had a strange smile on her face.

"Why is it always so good with you, and so bad every time I try it with someone I know? I get all tense and tight and I can't relax and nothing happens."

"It will, give yourself time. Some things take practice."

"I'll practice with you every night for ten years!"

"And never get pregnant?"

"There are ways."

"And none of them work, all the time."

"They will for me."

"How old are you?"

"Twenty."

"And your father doesn't think there's a man in the whole county who is good enough for you?"

"How did you know? I've had two suitors this year, and Daddy threw both of them off the ranch. I saw one of them in town, but he was so scared of Daddy that he wouldn't even talk to me."

Spur kissed her. "Give it another year, until you're twenty-one. Then move to town, or in to Portland and tell your old man to go to hell."

She grinned. "I'd love to do that. One of my brothers did. Then he came back."

She sat up, threw off the sheet and began kissing his chest.

"Again! Again! I don't want to waste another minute!"

"You want to see a soft little worm?"

She looked at his crotch. "Oh, the poor little darling!"

"Make him well again."

Maggie knew exactly what to do. Two minutes

later her head bobbed up from his crotch and she laughed softly.

"He's standing up and raring to go." She rolled over and got up on her hands and knees.

"The first animals I ever saw fucking were dogs. Do me this way, darling Spur! I've never fucked dog fashion before!"

Spur knelt behind her. "You're sure?"

"Just hit the right hole!"

Spur lifted and probed a moment, then slid into her and leaned over her grabbing a hanging breast with each hand. He stroked and felt his staff rubbing against her clit. After a dozen probes she climaxed and wobbled and vibrated and moaned. Halfway through she lost her balance and fell on her stomach on the bed. Spur rode her down and the climax left her gasping for air. Then she laughed.

"Guess we fell down."

"I like it this way. Okay?"

"Sure, it's different."

He started moving again and felt her respond and soon he was shooting the moon and riding the cloud trails until he shot his last load and sagged down on top of her, catching his weight with his elbows and knees.

"You are wild!" she said. Then she cried.

He moved and turned her so he could hold her. The sobs came and she blubbered for five minutes. Spur knew there was nothing he could do but wait. When she tapered off and the sobs turned into an occasional gasp, he kissed her forehead.

"Now, tell me about it, Margaret Smith."

She sighed and looked up at him. "You're a man, you wouldn't understand."

"Let me try."

She scowled, took a deep breath. "Well, it's just that I want to get married so damn bad! Daddy doesn't understand. He thinks things should be done a certain way, at a certain time. He says I should wait until I'm twenty-two to get married, so I'll be settled down.

"Bullshit! I want a man now! I want somebody I can take to bed every night for two years if he'll have me. I want to get fucked until I'm so sore that I can hardly pee. I'm a woman. I'm the only woman in the ranch house and Daddy just doesn't understand."

She gasped a pair of times as the crying jag was playing itself out. He kissed her cheek.

"And so?"

"And so, I want to tell Daddy that I'm going to move into town and stay with my aunt here, so I can meet men and find one to marry. I don't care if he doesn't own half of Oregon. I don't care if he's a clerk in a store or runs a railroad some- where. I just want to find my man, the man I'm supposed to love and have babies with. My father simply can't understand that."

"Have you talked with your aunt about it? Maybe the two of you could persuade him. Invite him in to your aunt's house and you come and tell him what you want. Does he have a cook at the ranch?"

"Yes. And one of the ranch hand's wife is housekeeper. He doesn't need me out there."

"So do it. Talk to your aunt tomorrow before you go back, get it set up for this week. The Land Grant thing is going to be over in a week or so. Don't worry about it."

She sat up, wiped the tears from her eyes and

off her cheeks, and urged him up. Then she hugged him so tight he thought she was going to crack a rib.

"Love you, love you, love you! You have helped me tonight more than you'll ever know! Now, while you rest up, I'll fix the snack. I can't expect you to do all this tough physical exercise without providing you with some nourishment. I know you ate up my titties, but this is better for you."

He sat there as she jumped out of bed as bare as the day she was born, found a sack at the side of the dresser and laid out on top a picnic of cut apples, wedges of cheese, chunks of fresh baked bread and a bottle of wine.

"Now, this is what I call service," Spur said. They stood at the dresser and nibbled on the cheese and bread, ate the apple sections and sipped at the wine.

"Don't eat everything!" She said sharply. "We have to save some for our three A.M. snack."

"How are you going to wake up at three o'clock," he asked.

Maggie laughed and nibbled at his ear. "You foolish man. You didn't think I was going to waste any time tonight sleeping, did you? Now hurry up, I'm getting curious about how we're going to do our fuck-fuck the next time."

Spur downed the last of the wine in his glass and slapped her on the bottom.

"Yes!" she said squealing softly. "Spank me! Not too hard but just hard enough. That really gets me all hot and ready! Come on, right now, I have been a bad girl and you need to spank me until my little bottom turns all red!"

He did.

Then he lifted her legs on his shoulders and

drove into her so hard and fast that she yelped in surprise, then she wailed.

"You touched something deep inside me!" she said. "It felt so unusual, so weird and wild. Do it again!"

They had their snack at two-thirty instead of three, and made love twice after that and Spur McCoy watched her dress and get ready to leave at four.

"Darling, I'll go back to Paula's house and sleep until noon, just in case Daddy stops by. But soon I'll be living full time in town, or in Portland."

She knelt on the bed and kissed him, then hugged him tightly.

"Spur McCoy, I'll never know how to thank you. She flashed him a perky smile from those big brown eyes, then slipped out of his room.

Spur checked his pocket watch. It was four-thirty. He turned over and slept until eight.

13

That same night, Colette Paris closed her third round of singing at the Sagebrush Saloon with a haunting, touching love song, *My True, True Love*. A young cowboy waited for her in her dressing room. When she opened the door, Colette stopped suddenly, her hand to her mouth in fright.

"Oh, no, Colette, don't be frightened. I just wanted to tell you how wonderful you sang tonight. You were better than anybody I've ever heard in Chicago! Really you sing just beautiful."

She began to edge back toward the bar.

"Come in, Colette. I'm Hank, from the triple R. Mean you no harm. Lordy no! Just want to be here with you a minute or two, is that too much to ask?"

"You surprised me, Hank. I'm usually not so touchy. It was nice talking to you. Now I need to rest. I always rest a few minutes after each performance."

"I could wait just outside. I thought maybe we

could talk a while. Be more than glad to walk you back to your hotel. Heard you stay at the Grande Ronde. That's a nice hotel. I never stayed there.''

"Hank, it was sweet of you to come back and see me, but now I really do have to sit down for a few minutes, alone. Would you go back to the bar, please?''

Hank, a cowboy about five feet eight, grinned, turned his brown low crowned hat in his hands and bobbed his head.

"Yes, Miss Colette, I most certainly will. Anything you ask, that's what I'm gonna do just quicker than a spring calf finding his mama.'' He moved toward the door. He stopped beside her.

Colette shivered.

"Oh, Miss Colette, would you mind my giving you just a little kiss on the cheek?''

"Yes, I would mind!'' She said it sharply.

Hank shrugged. "Figures. Don't hurt none to ask. I'll wait out in the bar if you want me to walk you to your hotel. Sure hope you do. Some rough, mean no-a-counts roam around this time of night out there on the street.'' He touched one finger to his forehead in a kind of salute and went out the door. Colette closed the door and leaned against it.

For a minute she thought she was going to cry. Then she fought back the emotion and sat in the chair and carefully wiped off most of the traces of makeup she used around her eyes and on her lips and cheeks. It was not blatant color like the saloon girls used. She was not a saloon girl. She was a singer!

It took her ten minutes to stop her shaking. She took a quick drink from a small flask of brandy.

Someone knocked on her door.

"Yes?"

"Lefty, you okay? Saw some guy trying to sneak back here."

She opened the door.

"Somebody was in here when I came back. Hank. I got rid of him. He scared me, Lefty."

"I'll watch your dressing room better," he said. "You want Billy to walk you to the hotel?"

"No, that's silly. I'll be fine. I'm almost ready to go."

Lefty nodded and left.

She checked her small windup clock on the dressing table. It was eleven fifteen. Colette put on a small hat, took her reticule with her hotel key, and went out to the bar. She did not see Hank among the dozen or so patrons. She waved at Lefty and walked out the door.

Hank waited for her half a block down. It was too far to run back to the bar.

"Evening, Miss Colette. I was going this way, mind if I walk along?"

"Boardwalks are made for everyone."

"I figured as how."

"Did I tell you I'm from Chicago? Grew up in the city and now I'm a cowboy. Isn't that strange? Always wanted to come out west. This is about as far as you can get."

Colette decided she would go straight to the clerk when she got to the hotel. If Hank was still there the clerk would take care of him. He had done it once before for her.

Hank talked about Chicago as they walked. He continued up the steps and right into the hotel.

Nobody stood behind the clerk's desk.

No one was in the lobby.

"Thank you, Hank, for seeing me safely home.

I'll be fine now. Goodnight.''

"Goodnight, Miss Colette.''

She turned and walked away. She was at the top of the flight of steps to the second floor before she realized he was right behind her.

"No, Hank, go away or I'm going to scream.''

"Now, pretty, great singing little Colette, you wouldn't want to do that.''

He stepped up beside her, caught her arm in a firm grip and walked with her down the hall. He knew which room was hers and stopped at the door.

"Open it, Colette. I could kick it open but you don't want that, do you?''

She couldn't talk. Slowly Colette took the key from her purse and put it in the keyhole. Hank turned it, opened the door and took the key out. He walked her inside the room, and closed the door.

He snapped a match into flame and held her as he moved to the lamp on the dresser. A moment later the lamp burned brightly as he adjusted the wick.

She had stood where he left her.

"Now, isn't this cozy?'' He said. He went to the door and locked it, pocketing the key.

"Miss Colette, you and me are going to get to know each other one hell of a lot better. He grabbed her chin in his hand and his fingers pinched her cheeks painfully. "And don't think that I'm afraid to hurt that sweet little body of yours to get what I want. You know what that is.''

He turned her to him and kissed her lips, a hard, demanding kiss. She didn't respond.

"Little Colette, I'm gonna fuck you, you know

that now. I'm gonna fuck you half a dozen times until I can't get my prick up stiff anymore, and you're going to love every stroke of it. Now, let's get busy and get you out of all of those clothes.''

He grabbed the top of her dress. ''You want me to rip this thing off you?''

''No! No. I'll take it off.''

''Don't look so scared, pretty pussy. You've been in bed with lots of men. You like to fuck as well as you like to sing. Just think that you invited me up instead of the other way, and then you'll enjoy getting banged and sucking me off as much as I will.''

Slowly she undid the snaps and buttons on the dress and pulled it over her head. Her mind was whirling. What could she do? She was frantic. She wasn't a virgin, having sex with the man did not bother her, but the idea that he was forcing her to do it made her furious.

She had to think of something. What? After he had climaxed! Yes, when he was exhausted and his guard was down. She would do it then. He would not be expecting anything. She would smile and pretend that she was *enjoying* having sex with him. Oh, God! Was she that good at acting? she had to be. He could kill her right there if he suspected.

Colette watched him unbuttoning his shirt. For a moment a picture flashed in front of her eyes of another man taking off his shirt. It was in her family house in Portland, Maine. The buttons came off and she saw the manly chest and she heard someone scream. She had screamed that day and ran from the house but he caught her in the woods in back of the house.

''Hey, you gonna undress, or I got to help?''

She shook her head to come back to the present and lifted the chemise over her head. She did not wear a binder, that long strip of cloth to keep her breasts from bouncing. She hated them. Now her big breasts bounced and jiggled as she dropped the chemise.

"Oh, yeah, big tits. I bet the guys you had big boobies. They look like they need chewing on."

He lunged across the room, fondled her a minute, then bent and sucked one of her big breasts into his mouth. He was vunerable right now. If she had a heavy knife she could plunge it in his back.

He came away, grinned at her and went down on her other breast.

"Damnit, get the rest of your clothes off!" he said between bites on her boobs. "Hurry up!"

She opened the buttons on her drawers, and pulled down her last protection, the knee length underpants. He pushed her on the bed and stripped the cotton garment off her legs, then grinned the way her legs had spread. She pulled them together and he laughed.

Quickly he pulled off his boots and his pants. His penis was hard and slanting out at her, the head large and now purple with the engorging, hot blood.

"Oh, yeah!" he said softly. "There is nothing so good as nookie, good old pussy, cunt all naked and waiting on a bed. Yeah, in bed with your shoes off!

She spread her skirt to the side and folded it.

"What you doing?"

"You're so slow that I'm just being neat."

"I can get faster!" He pushed her flat on the

bed away from her skirt and spread her legs with his feet.

"Now, sweet little pussy, just how good are you?" He drove between her legs probing, searching. When he found the right spot she was dry. He swore, spit into his hand and wiped the saliva over his penis, then probed again.

He drove in hard and she screeched in pain.

"Easy!" she yelped.

"You wanted it fast, this is fast!" He made no attempt to satisfy her, simply powered into her, thrusting hard and long, his breath starting to come in furious pants as he rocked back and forth on his elbows and his knees.

She felt the soft glow begin to spread through her body and fought against it. This was not like last night. No! This was rape and she was furious! With her hand she grabbed the edge of her skirt and worked it slowly toward her. He noticed.

"I like to touch my clothes, makes me feel better."

He pulled the skirt against her side and then grunted and wailed in pure joy as he climaxed. He was panting and spent as he dropped on top of her. She used her right hand, worked through her skirt until she found the pocket.

Carefully she pulled the object from her skirt's hidden pocket and lifted it over Hank's back. With her left hand she reached up and quietly unfolded the four-inch knife blade and heard the brace lock in place.

"Whatcha doing?" Hank mumbled. "Damn that was fine!"

Colette lifted the knife, holding it firmly in her right hand and drove it down toward his left side.

She aimed it just under his ribs and pushed the blade into the hilt, then turned it and tried to rip it out.

Hank did the work for her, springing away from her only to collapse on his back on the bed.

Colette's eyes flared, her lips came open and she swung the bloody knife downward, ramming it between ribs into his chest. Hank looked at her once in disbelief, then his eyes rolled upward.

She drove the knife into his chest a dozen more times aiming for his heart. At last he stopped twitching.

She sat there on the bed, his bloody body in front of her. For a moment she wanted to vomit, then she pushed back the feeling and sprang to her feet. She put the pillow from the bed on the floor, then rolled him off the bed onto the pillow. She pulled the pillow and tugged at him, scooting him across the six feet to the alley window.

Quietly she lifted the window and peered out. No one was in the alley. She pushed his feet upward the twenty-four inches to the open window and forced them out. By struggling and shoving with all her strength she got him halfway out the window. Then she squatted over his head, grabbed his shoulders and straining every muscle in her legs and back, she heaved his torso up and forward.

Hank slid out the window, turned halfway over and hit the ground of the alley below.

Colette panted for a moment, sat on the floor looking at the room. The pillow had absorbed most of the blood from his body. There were few spots on the hardwood floor to clean up.

The sheets! They were covered with blood. Quickly she wrapped them up, washed off a spot of blood on the cheap mattress, and then checked out the window. She threw the sheets out as far down the alley as she could, then dressed and checked the linen closet down the hall. She found two fresh sheets, a pillow and a pillow case.

As quickly as she could she made the bed, cleaned off the knife and put it away in her skirt pocket. Then she slipped into her nightgown and lay in the bed.

He had deserved to die. He was as bad as all the rest of them! She blew out the lamp and lay in the darkness, her breath coming more naturally now and her furiously beating heart settling down.

It was over.

She could sleep now.

An hour later she had the same dream. She was being chased by a man. She ran out of the small house into the trees, but still the man came after her. Colette tried every way she could to get away but he countered her until at last he caught her.

Slowly, he took off her clothes and forced her to do all kinds of sexual acts with him. Again and again it happened, then one day she had a large folding knife in her skirt pocket. Just after he had raped her, she surprised him and slashed his throat, then cut him again and again and again.

She woke up with a start just as she slashed his neck. Colette was sweating and crying. She washed her face, and dried it. The man had been her brother, and she had been thirteen at the time. She would never forget it. But also, she would never be without that same four-inch folding knife.

It was well into the morning when a banging on her door wakened her. Colette got up, put on a robe and went to the door.

"Yes, who is it?"

"Sheriff Younger, Miss. Could I talk to you a minute?"

She said of course and opened the door.

He barely looked at her, instead looked at her bed.

"Interested to see which bed doesn't have any sheets. Nothing to be worried about. Little thing like you just couldn't have done it. Sorry I bothered you."

The sheriff turned and went down the hall to the next room.

She closed the door, not really understanding. She had the dream again last night. By now reality and the dream had merged and flowed together, until she could not tell which was fact and which was memory. She remembered the man who came to her room, but after that the man began to look like her brother and soon all she could see was her older brother who had been nineteen.

Colette, took a deep breath. She was hungry, she wanted to have a bath, and then have a good breakfast and take a long ride somewhere. At least she had learned to ride a horse on this Western trip. She loved to ride.

Colette looked at a red stain on the window sill. She got some water and a cloth and wiped it up. She wondered how that red mark got there.

14

Victor White had been working the south forty of his homestead when the three riders came over the ridge. The south forty had been laboriously plowed with a single bottom hand held plow and a mule, and he was ready to float it down with a tough oak log he had cut especially for the job. He wiped sweat off his forehead and looked up from where he had hitched the mule to the single tree that hooked the mule's harness to the log.

"Hold it right there, sodbuster!" The angry shout came from one of the riders who had out his six-gun and aimed it at Victor.

"No cause for firearms," Victor said. "Ain't got one on me. What can I do for you gents?"

"For starters, unhitch that mule and drive him back to your cabin. Got plans for you."

Victor spat a stream of tobacco juice into the plowed ground.

"Figure not. I got to get me this forty floated down by sundown so I can plant tomorrow. Getting late as it is."

The gunshot boomed in the morning air and the slug slammed into the sod an inch from Victor's boot.

"No time for arguments, sodbuster. You want the next one in your head or your heart?"

"He mean it?" Victor asked the man on the horse ten feet away.

"Damn right, move the mule or die where you stand."

"You boys usually ride for the RimRock outfit, as I recall. Wade sent you?"

"Never heard of any RimRock Ranch, said the first man who held the gun. "Now move it before I get unhappy."

Ten minutes later Victor slapped the reins on the back of the mule and prodded the sterile creature back to the tiny farm yard of his homestead just off the banks of the Grande Ronde river.

He saw three other men at the cabin. His wife, Etta, was loading up the wagon with things from the house.

"What is this?" Victor asked.

The big man from the roan horse had swung down, but stll held his weapon on Victor. He took three steps toward the homesteader and slammed his gloved fist into Victor's jaw. The farmer-rancher spun around and lost his balance and fell in the dirt.

"Victor, no more dumb-assed questions. You have half an hour to load anything you want to keep on that wagon over there. Then hitch your mule to it, climb on board and hightail it out of the county. We're running you off your place, case you are too stupid to figure it out."

"My homestead!"

"No way to prove that. Land office records all
burned up, didn't they? You've got twenty-eight
minutes left. You better hurry. And don't try to
get to a hidden gun. We've got six men and
twelve guns, including six rifles. You want to go
up against that much hot lead?"

"No." He hesitated. "You promise you won't
hurt Emma or the boys?"

"Nobody gets hurt long as you do as you're
told. Now get!"

The men on horseback walked their mounts
around the small "proved up" cabin watching the
tight-lipped Etta White push boxes of goods into
the wagon. She soon ran out of boxes and used
pillow cases to hold clothes. At last she rushed
back and forth and threw loose items into the
wagon box.

Victor helped for a while, then he hitched the
mule to the wagon and went back to the small
cabin. He had built it from logs hauled in from his
own land. Now strangers were running him off his
homestead. Five years he'd been here.

"Five minutes left," the big man on the roan
said.

"What about my cattle?" Victor asked.

"I don't see no cattle," another of the armed
men said.

"We find any strays with your brand, we'll
send them along to you," another guard said.

All the mounted men laughed.

Victor ran to the small lean-to that served as a
barn, and saddled his one cow pony. He tied a
lead line to a halter of a colt not yet six months
old and led him out of the small fenced pen.

"You call this a ranch with only one horse?"
one of the rousters said. "Damn, I wouldn't be

caught dead having a place like this.''

Etta looked at him with fire in her eyes.

"If I had got to my rifle in time, you would be dead!'' she spat at him.

The cowboy laughed, pointed his six-gun at her and said, "Bang, bang.'' Then they all laughed again.

"Time to move out,'' the leader said.

"Ain't got the bedstead yet,'' Victor said.

"Tough. Do it, boys.''

Two men ran inside the house.

"Get on the wagon, Smith, we're leaving. Get those two little brats too, wherever you've been hiding them.''

Etta called and two boys about five and six, ran from a patch of woods and jumped on the wagon.

"We going to town, mamma? Are we?''

"Yes, now hush.''

Victor looked at the cabin he has worked so hard to build and saw smoke coming from the front door.

"No!'' He roared. He jumped off the wagon and ran for the house. A lariat snaked out, circled his shoulders and jolted him to such a quick stop that he fell to the ground.

"Nooooooooooo!'' he screamed.

A pistol round dug up dirt beside him and the sharp report seemed to bring him out of his frenzy. Victor stood, brushed off the dust from his work clothes, then walked around the semicircle of mounted men and looked searchingly at each face. Only then did he climb on the wagon and pick up the reins to the mule. The horse and colt followed on a lead line tied to the wagon.

"I got me a good memory for faces. Just want to tell you I'll never forget a one of your looks.

You'll be hearing from me one of these days. You owe me one homestead, a cabin and my livelihood. You'll be hearing from me!"

Etta sat on a cushion in the front of the wagon, her long skirt hiked up to show her ankles. She didn't care. She let the tears come then. She would not watch the cabin burn. Smoke came from both broken out windows now and the front and back doors. It would be nothing but a pile of ashes the next time she saw it. It had been a good five years.

"What are we going to do, Victor? What in the world are we going to do?"

"First off we go to La Grande and see the sheriff. If he can't do anything, I get myself a rifle and come back to my land. Any man who sets foot on it gets his head blown off!"

The warm spring sun had just passed its zenith, when Victor White and his family drew their wagon up in front of the Wallowa County courthouse and the sheriff's office. Another wagon sat nearby with a woman and four children in it. Victor tied the reins and jumped down.

"Take care what you say, Victor," Etta cautioned.

He hurried off toward the sign over the door to the sheriff's office. Inside he found Sheriff Quincy Younger talking with a man obviously right off the farm in his bib overalls and narrow brimmed hat.

"Just won't stand for it, Sheriff! You got to do something about that damned triple R bunch of thieves!"

"Mr. Nelson, I understand the problem. I'll get out there and see what I can do. Can you identify the men that run you off your property?"

"Hell, yes! Man never forgets faces of men who do that."

"Sheriff," Victor said. "Six RimRock Ranch hands drove me and my family off our place, too. Then they burned down my house. I want to charge them with arson and anything else we can come up with. Better get a posse, there's thirty men on that spread and they all got six-guns and rifles."

Sheriff Younger looked up. "Victor White isn't it? You said some of Wade Smith's hands forced you off your place, too? That makes three this morning. What the hell is he trying to do?"

"Easy what he's up to, Sheriff. He claims he worked that valley of mine for twenty years before I come. Says he owns it by rights of development. Them hands as much as told me he was taking back what was rightly his. With all the land office records burned up, how can I prove that the land is mine? I proved up on that eighty acres!"

Spur McCoy eased in the sheriff's office. He motioned the sheriff to one side of the room to talk.

"That makes three, Younger. We better move."

"Go see Wade Smith?"

"Right now. I'd suggest two more men and you and I. We leave the men run off their land here in town. We don't want any hotheads on this side. Can you go?"

"Half an hour. Have a rifle and six-gun and we'll take a ride."

They made the ride in under two hours, met a guard at the gate who led them down the long lane to the big ranch house. Wade Smith was on the porch waiting for them when they rode up. He did not invite them to get off their horses.

"What the hell you want, Younger?"

"Three families have been burned out and run off their homesteads near your ranch. What do you know about it?"

"Not a damned thing."

"Watch your tongue, Smith!" the sheriff barked. "I have evidence enough right now to charge you and a dozen or more of your men with arson, rustling and a half dozen other crimes. Just watch how you talk."

"I don't know a thing about anyone being chased off their homesteads. But I do know that I own land where some of these families have been squatting. Over twenty years ago I bought this land from the Yakima nation. Paid them with beef and salt and provisions for two years. I have witnesses."

"Then you admit you run off these three families?"

"Don't know what you're talking about."

"Your riders did it, Smith. And they don't do anything without orders from you. We can identify every man on the three raiding parties. You can't afford to let them all run. You'll pay for everything you destroyed, Smith, and you'll rebuild those houses, better than before."

"You made a fatal mistake, Mr. Smith," Spur McCoy said. "Just because the local land office burned down, don't think all of the records were destroyed. All such records are made out in triplicate. One copy goes to Washington, D.C. and two are kept by the local office. Those records are still safe and can be used at any time."

"McCoy, I told you to get off my land once."

"And I told you I'd come back anytime I wanted to. I told the sheriff we should arrest you right now. He said to give you one more chance."

"He's got to get elected again here, you don't, McCoy."

"One more incident, Smith, just one more homesteader gets run off land near your ranch, and I'll come out here and take you back to town for trial, and fifty guards around your house won't stop me. Remember, the attacker always has the advantage."

"I'm scared, fast gun, just damn scared," Smith said. "You better worry about that con man of an Englishman. I heard about his plan to take over the county. I saw his kind before, in Boston thirty years ago."

"The courts will settle that," Sheriff Younger said. "The three families you burned out will be settled by me, and damn soon. Now, will you agree to stop this taking the law into your own hands until the courts settle the Englishman's Royal Claim?"

"That could take months!"

"Two weeks at the most," Spur said. "If I can prove that Sir Jeffrey Mountbatten is a fraud and perhaps a murderer, it could be settled in a day or two."

"Good, I'll let you make your play. But just remember this whole end of the valley is mine! I've developed it, I've grazed it for twenty years!"

"Grazing public land doesn't make it yours, Smith. You know nothing about the law. Get a good lawyer and ask him for some advice. You're going to need it." Spur turned his mount and the other three moved with him.

They rode slowly away from the buildings and down the long lane. The guard did not come with them.

"Don't look back," Spur said so the other three could hear. "We've stopped him. He won't run off any more homesteaders. Now we have to talk to the survivors and get statements and any identification they can make. Descriptions at least of the riders. Eighteen of them. There must be a way to identify those men with certainty."

The sheriff scratched his chin. "Sure as hell gonna try. This kind of range warfare I don't want in the county. The big ranchers have too much power now. Let Smith get away with this and there will be no way to hold him. We have to stop him dead in his saddle right now!"

15

Wade Smith watched the sheriff and the three men ride off his ranch. He called his foreman over and gave him curt instructions, then Wade went back in the house.

When the owner of the RRR came out five minutes later, he was ready for the range. He left with twelve men, four of them heading in three different directions. They carried the equipment they would need.

Wade went with the group nearest his ranch headquarters, a long arm of land that he had neglected to buy from the government when he had a chance before the homesteader moved in five years ago. The eighty acres bordered the river and controlled access to a half mile long stretch that he needed.

He sat on his big gelding at the small rise and looked down on the piece of land he wanted and he would have it! First he had a small job to do.

The four cowboys spread out on a sweep down the quarter mile wide stretch of land pushing all the cattle they could find in front of them. The land was open, part of the glacial formed four mile wide depression that had attracted a river.

The cattle were not the best, a few longhorn mix and the general range cattle of Eastern Oregon.

Wade was not so interested in improving his herd as eliminating that of a competitor. When the homesteader returned to his land, if he won in the courts, he would find no house, no barn, no buildings of any kind and no cattle.

The owner of the RimRock Ranch estimated there might be two hundred animals in the small strip of land. It was lush grazing land and could support that many. He would drive them north, past the edge of the man's property, toward a box canyon well beyond his own ranch boundary and into federal land.

The cowboys knew their jobs. The smart cutting horses could anticipate every move of a steer or a cow and calf and turn at just the precise moment to move the animal the way the rider indicated.

In an hour the cowboys had rounded up every critter and bunched them. Then they began the slow process of driving them north. The animals did not want to leave the good grass, nor the handy drinking water.

Wade looked in wonder at the quality of some of the stock. He was surprised. They all carried a brand, the FP ranch. Wade laughed when he figured how easy a running iron could change that brand into his own RRR. And that was exactly what he had in mind.

They got the critters into the box canyon early and immediately bunched them. Two men started

a fire and threw in the long running irons. One
iron was simply a right angle bend in a straight
piece of steel so it could be used to form straight
lines. Another iron from the RRR would make the
rounded section of the "R." A third iron was the
"R" from the regular branding tools.

At the site of the fire, Wade stepped down from
his horse. He had spent years in the saddle, and
could do any job on his ranch better than his men.
That bred respect for the boss. He checked the
fire and the irons, then when they were glowing
red hot, he signalled the ropers.

They picked out a steer and began the ballet of
roping. Wade insisted his men use the head and
heel catch. The first roper used an overhand
throw of his lariat to catch the head of the steer.
He tightened the line and led the critter away.

The second roper came up behind the steer and
made a heel catch on the back two legs using a
sidearm cast. This slipped the rope under the
steer's back feet. The rider pulled up the noose
and held the steer. They slowly stretched out the
steer by pulling on both ends. Since both rear legs
were noosed together, the animal soon lost its
balance and fell on its side.

Now it was ready for branding or castration or
any other attention needed.

Wade walked up to the first thrown steer and
looked at it. The owner's hip brand the FP
showed plainly. He checked for other marks and
found only a small ear notch. There was no jaw
brand or wattle mark or road brand. Wade
smiled.

"Brand them," he said. And make a fresh ear
cut over that small one. There won't be a fair day
in hell anybody'll be able to say these cattle

aren't regular triple R stock."

The branding began. Soon the thrashing cattle turned the area around the fire into a barren, dusty arena. Red hot irons seared the flesh, burned hair off and left a triple R brand on the animal's hip, the owner brand.

Deftly the running iron put a curved line around the end of the "F" and created the top half of the "R." The running iron lanced a line down from the loop to complete the "R." Sometimes the "R" branding iron was set directly over the old letters to create new ones. When the expert branders were done the ear was clipped removing the old ear mark with that of the RRR.

Then the bawling calf, steer, bull or cow was untied and two cowboys herded it into a new holding area.

They worked until it was too dark to see the brands. Half the cattle had been marked. They rolled out blankets and slept. They would go to work again as soon as it was dawn and be finished before noon. Then they would return to their normal duties.

Wade left the branding at dusk and rode to the other branding site where the smaller herds from the other two homesteaders he had burned out had been gathered. There were only about fifty head, and they had all been branded and would be driven to the major holding box canyon at daylight.

Wade thought of the sheriff and he snorted. Anyway it turned out, he won. Nobody would be able to identify any cattle. He might have to rebuild the buildings he burned down, but the cattle he took were worth much more than three shacks.

He rode back to his ranch with his foreman and three cowboys from the last branding. It had been a good day's work.

Later, Wade leaned back in his big rocking chair on the porch and watched the moon glinting off the Grande Ronde river. Why in hell hadn't he sired any sons? What does a man build up a big ranch for? He had no intentions of giving the place to some snot nosed kid who Margaret just happened to marry. She had about as much sense in judging men as a heifer in heat.

If his wife hadn't died so young . . .

He could always marry again, find some young, wide-hipped woman with big tits who could produce two or three sons for him in three years. An idea. A good brood bitch was what he needed, but where did a man find one in La Grande?

Virginia came out on the porch and sat in the other rocker.

"Daddy, I've been thinking about moving into town. I am away from everything out here."

"No."

"Daddy, you can't run my life for me. I want to go places and do things. I've never been out of the county! Do you realize that? I want to go visit my aunt in Portland. I'm going to write her a letter and ask her if I can come. I'll stay a month and then come back."

"Absolutely not!"

"Why?"

"Don't have to give you a reason, you're my daughter."

"I'm a grown woman. Lots of the girls I used to know from church are married. One has four children already! Do you want me to be an old maid!"

"Virginia. You stand to inherit this whole spread some day. And the man you marry will get it as a gift. I want to be sure you marry a good man."

"I don't want your old ranch! Sell it. Move to San Francisco and you can go to the whorehouse every night instead of just on Saturday nights the way you do now!"

Virginia jumped up and flounced away.

Wade watched her go and only with a great effort did he hold his angry words. Slowly he began to smile. So she did know where he went on Saturday afternoons. Good. But that also meant that she was a grown up woman. He would have to think about what to do with her. It might be a good idea to let her stay in town for a while. Then she would forget about Portland.

Portland was out of the question. She'd get married and bring home some city feller who would ruin the ranch in five years. Maybe he should sell it. What was he killing himself for to make the triple R bigger and bigger?

Wade slapped his hand down on his dusty denim pants leg. "Hell, just to do it!" he said outloud. Just to prove to everyone else in the valley that he was smarter and meaner and a better rancher than they would ever be. That was enough.

Hell, it didn't make that much difference what happened to the triple R. When he was in a pine box six feet under the ground it wouldn't matter a whit!

Wade stood slowly and walked through the

night toward the small house to the left of the ranchhouse where his cook for the past ten years had lived. Her name was Mildred and she had been his foreman's wife before the man got gored by a range bull. Wade promised him to keep Mildred as cook before he died.

He watched and saw no one in sight. He slipped in the back door of the four room place and called.

"Milly?"

"Yes, Wade. I'm in the bedroom."

He went in and saw her at the mirror combing her long black hair. She turned and smiled. Milly was forty, and enjoyed eating her own cooking. She was short and heavy with huge breasts that sagged from their weight. Her small, round face had bright blue eyes, pink cheeks and a smile that charmed every hand on the place. She had almost married one three years ago, but he drifted off when he found out Milly was barren.

Milly turned. She wore a soft cotton nightgown.

"Problems, Wade?"

"A few. I just got to thinking about the ranch, and Virginia, and what the hell I'm doing all of this work for."

"Tell me all about it." She put down her comb, stood and walked to him. Her breasts bulged the nightgown. She unbuttoned his shirt and slipped it off.

"Want me to heat up some water? Only take a half hour or so. That would give us plenty of time. Later you can have a fine bath."

He nodded, then reached out and caught one big breast with each hand.

"Christ! but you feel good."

"It's been almost a month, Wade."

"I know." He massaged her breasts, then kissed her. He came away. "I'll get the fire going."

He used kindling and then bigger wood to get the fire started in the wood stove, then moved the copper boiler on top of the stove and Milly poured in two buckets of well water.

Wade stoked the fire again, then Milly pushed against him, and began unbuttoning his pants.

"Right here in the kitchen, woman?"

"Any place as long as you got it hard!" she said and smiled.

They hurried to the bedroom and she undressed him, then slid out of the nightgown. She was fat, her large breasts sagged and Ward laughed and rolled her on the bed.

"I'll take comfort over speed any day," he said and began licking her breasts.

Milly purred softly. "I've got some surprises for you tonight, Wade," she said. "Something that we've never done. I think you'll like it."

"Woman, that's got to be during our fourth or fifth fuck. I've got plans myself before that. You'll have to wait your turn to choose."

"I'll wait," she said and reached for his crotch.

Upstairs in the big house, Virginia watched the lights come on in the kitchen of the cook's house. Then the light went off as the lamp must have been carried into the bedroom.

She knew her father was there. Good. She liked Milly, who had been like a mother to her the last ten years. Milly had told her about her bleeding time, and sat up with her for hours one night when it finally happened, talking to her, soothing her when she cried.

Virginia wondered about the new hand they

had taken on. He was not much over twenty, had sandy hair and was tall and sturdy. He spoke with a funny accent. He said was from New York. She had liked him the first time she saw him.

But she knew better than to let on. If her father had even the smallest inkling what she was thinking, he would run the man off the ranch. No, she would take her time, see how he fit in with the crew, and then, one day, maybe, when there was no one around she could get a note to him.

They could meet down by the river. For just a moment she wondered how it would be. Then she was off in a fantasy. She lay on the bed and when she thought of his hands touching her, she touched herself. He was so bold as to rub her breasts, but she said it was all right.

Virginia rubbed her own breasts. His hands wandered then, and so did hers and then he was over her and she was on her back, her knees spread and raised, and he was entering her!

She found the candle in her nightstand and put saliva on it and lowered it between her legs and then surged upward against it as it slid into her hot, wet slit.

"Oh, yes! yes!" she murmured as her finger found her hard little clit and she stroked it.

"Yes, darling, so good!"

Then the ranch boy was lost in her thoughts and it was Spur McCoy over her and stroking into her and she was overcome with emotion as he reached her climax.

Five minutes later she smiled into the darkness.

"Lovely, Spur McCoy, just fantastic. I won't let you get away so easily the next time."

16

When Spur McCoy, the sheriff and his two deputies were on the way back to La Grande after talking to Wade Smith, they found a strange group just outside of town. It was a smartly outfitted democratic buggy with four horsemen riding shotgun. When they came up to the group, the guards saw the sheriff and relaxed.

Inside the buggy sat Lord Jeffrey Mountbatten and his manservant Edward Long.

"Sheriff, just the man I wish to see," Lord Mountbatten said. "The tenor of the population has quieted and now seems to be fairly stable. The people have accepted the idea that the courts will decide in their favor, so the animosity toward me has reduced.

"However, as you can see, I am taking no chances. I don't want to get shot dead and then win the judgment for all of this beautiful land and not be able to enjoy it."

"Seems the folks have quieted down after the first panic, Mr. Mountbatten," the sheriff said.

"You might be a lord and knighted in your country, but that don't mean a damn thing here, Mountbatten. You obey our laws or you get your neck stretched. That good and plain enough?"

"Truly my good man. We have sheriff's in England as well. I understand your position. But I also wish you to understand mine. Just because I own the whole county, it is still a political entity of Oregon and the United States, and must be governed as such. I'll only be the freeholder of the land and buildings. Laws will still apply, the city and county governments still exist.

"I totally understand all of this, my good fellow. I've been looking over some of my land. It is vast, much larger in reality than it looked on the map. Yes, it will take me days, perhaps weeks to visit all of it."

"No need to do that until the court makes up its mind about that document of yours," Spur said.

Mountbatten smiled at Spur. "And I understand Mr. McCoy is a lawman of some repute engaged by the United States Government. That all is quite impressive. I expect to cooperate completely with the government entities and to participate in the governing function wherever needed.

"I really see no practical purpose to disposses anyone from any land or building. Quite simply only the ownership will change hands. I am working out some applicable share cropper tenant basis for the farms, ranches and businesses. An equitable plan I assure you, Sheriff, that should keep everyone happy.

"Perhaps later the living units will be assessed some type of rent, I'm not sure yet. You see, gentlemen, as the Duke of Wallowa, I will rule in

a way. I was born to rule, to lead, and by God I
will do my best!"

He nodded to the sheriff and motioned for his
driver to move the rig on upstream along the
Grande Ronde river.

The sheriff watched the entourage move away.

"Something I don't like about that man,"
Younger said.

"Join a growing group," Spur said. "Somehow
he's too slick, too sure of himself. It's not the
British accent, there's something else there that
bothers me."

Back in town, Spur let the sheriff talk to the
dispossessed, and went back to the wreckage of
the burned out office. Basement and cellar were
still the key words. He probed the entire floor
area of the house with a steel rod, ramming it
hard into the ground to find any hidden basement
or hiding area.

After two hours he found nothing.

Spur saw the Englishman ride back into town
and go into the hotel. Spur went back there as
well, cleaned up and changed his shirt, and
walked up to the third floor to see the Duke of
Wallowa. Two guards stood in the hall.

"Tell Mr. Mountbatten that Spur McCoy is
here to see him."

One of the guards knocked on the door and
when it opened a crack he relayed the message.
The door came open fully.

Edward Long smiled at the Secret Service
agent.

"Mr. McCoy, of course, our Irish cousin. Won't
you come in? The Duke is in his room, he'll be out
shortly."

Lord Jeffrey came out at once. "Ah, Mr.

McCoy. Just cleaning up a little. What can we do for you?"

"Your ancestoral home in England. I was wondering where it is?"

"Actually it lay in Sheffield. My father became the Duke of Sheffield, the title I inherited."

"Interesting. Is there a castle and everything?"

"No, no. Just a manor house. It is quite extensive by local standards. It's on two square miles of wooded hills with a trout stream and a herd of deer. The house itself is thirty-six rooms with servants' quarters in another building. It's quite adequate."

"I would guess you have farm lands?"

"Oh, quite. All done on a sharecropper basis as you blokes would say. Perhaps I could ask you for some advice. You seem to be well traveled."

"Fire away."

"I understand there are great stands of virgin timber in my mountains in the Wallowas. Pine and fir. The pine is the prime lumber tree in this area. Would it be practical for me to start a logging or lumbering operation in the mountains?"

"Impossible. Whoever harvests that timber will need a railroad to get the logs or the lumber out to the markets. You can't haul logs out for sixty miles, and then get it from here to the railroad. It's just too far."

"Pity. I had the same conclusions. The nice thing about steers is that they have their own transportation devices, four feet."

"True, driving steers is much easier. That's why the big ranchers have developed here, not big lumberyards or sawmills."

"As you can see, sir. I am learning as I go along."

"All of us do, Mountbatten. Might I ask how you hope to establish the authenticity of your Royal Land Grant?"

"You may ask, but my barrister will have to answer. I engaged legal representation this afternoon."

"Sorry, I don't want to talk to a lawyer. Thank you, but I have an appointment and I must rush away. Maybe we can talk again sometime."

"Yes, I would enjoy that. I want to learn more about Washington, D.C., your capital."

Spur said goodbye and stepped into the hall. He was halfway down when a man arrived staring at each door number. Soon he found the right one with the two guards.

"I'm Bill Amos. I need to see Sir Jeffrey."

A moment later the man who was dressed in a Sunday suit entered the room. Spur frowned but continued on to his own room.

In the Englishman's room he had moved behind a small desk and now looked up at the new visitor.

"Ah, Mr. Amos. Have you considered my offer?"

"Yes, and I've about decided to go ahead." Amos was thin and nervous. He kept running his fingers back through his hair.

"Decided that I can get a deed from you now, I'll be free and clear if you win the court case. If the States won't honor your claim, then I still have my property."

"That's the La Grande Mercantile, isn't it Mr. Amos?"

"Yes, right. I have drawn up a bill of sale granting to me and my heirs or assignees all rights to the building and the land under it to me for the sum of two hundred dollars."

"We mentioned a figure of three hundred."

"That's a year's wages, Sir Jeffrey. All I can raise is two hundred, take it or leave it. That's all I can afford for this kind of insurance."

Mountbatten stalled. He walked to the window and was counting up the firms he could squeeze for two hundred each. If he could get twenty or thirty of them, they would ride out on horses in the dead of the night, take their money with them and catch the stage well out of town.

He came back to the desk.

"All right, Mr. Amos. I'll do it for you, if you will spread the word to those you can trust about this service. We can't let the general public hear about this. I'm dealing only with reputable businessmen of integrity such as you. Also we don't want the sheriff or the court involved. There is nothing at all illegal here, it's a matter of double insurance if you will."

"I understand. Just sign at these two places, and I sign under them."

"You did bring cash, Mr. Amos?"

"Just the way we talked about."

"Mostly ten dollar bills, is that all right?"

"Perfectly acceptable." He signed the papers. "Now, if you have one or two friends you can trust not to let this get out . . ."

"Yes, I think I should tell some friends. Should they contact you here?"

The Englishman counted the money, let it lay on the table and held out his hand.

"Mr. Amos, a pleasure helping you this way."

When the merchant had gone, Edward Long ran out of the connecting room and counted the bills.

"Glory be! What a good thing we got going here, guv'nor. I've got three more men waiting in the hall. They wouldn't say why they wanted to see you. Think I'll bring them in and put them in the spare bedroom so not anyone else will see them."

"Capital idea, old man. Now let's rush it. We could have ten visitors tonight! I told them anytime up to midnight."

By midnight the Duke of Wallowa was so excited and nervous he could hardly keep a straight face.

"The idiots!" he exclaimed softly when the last of the merchants had left. They had sold back property the men owned or had been paying mortgages on to fourteen men. All were properly glad to take the small risk. The amounts were from two hundred to three hundred, and Long had kept the tab and the cash.

Long came out of the bedroom with a flushed face, his eyes dancing.

"Gawd! I can't believe it. We've got three thousand five hundred American dollars in our kip!"

"Now this is a good night's work."

"Let's leave tonight! Let's get out of here while we still have our skulls in one piece, mate. These blokes are going to get on to us damn quick I've a hunch. We can rent horses and be ten miles out on the way to Portland when the stage comes along the road. We pay and get on board."

"Just the start, Edward, just the start. We can

do as well for three days and have ten thousand dollars!"

His eyes glinted at the idea. They locked the door and went into the bedroom and looked at the bills stacked on the bed.

Sir Jeffrey ripped off his shirt and began unbuttoning his pants.

"Money makes you horny, doesn't it you old cock!"

"Damn right. I want to lay in all that money naked! I want you to put it to me right on top of three thousand five hundred dollars!"

Jeffrey was naked, he fell on the bed on his back, then rolled over and lifted his bare ass into the air.

"Come on, Edward, ram it into me right now. This is one that I'll never forget. The day we made three thousand five hundred dollars and you buggered me right on top of all that cash."

"Fifty-fifty, you promised me."

"Damn right, now get your fly open and that delicious prick out and throw it into me. Now!"

Colette had sung beautifully that night. One of the clerks from the hardware store had stayed for both performances, and fell into step with her as she left the saloon.

"Miss Colette? I hope you don't mind if I walk with you to your hotel? I'm Gerry Todd."

"I'd rather you didn't, Mr. Todd."

"Call me Gery. That's okay. No problem. I'm going that way. Really appreciated your singing and playing. We come from Baltimore and there's performers there lots of times. But you were better than any of them I ever heard."

"Please don't walk with me, Mr. Todd."

"Come on, now Colette. I'd really appreciate it."

"I do have to make a short detour."

"No problem, I have time. Nobody waiting up for me."

"Oh."

They walked a block and she turned down a dark side street.

"I must see a woman down here."

"Fine, I'll go along."

When they came to the middle of the block she stopped.

"I didn't want anyone to see. Gerry, I like you. Would you like to kiss me?"

"What? Like to? Damn, I'd half kill to kiss you. Right here?"

"Nobody can see us. No houses or businesses open."

"Now?"

"Yes, now."

He kissed her and she held him tightly. When he started to move away, she opened her mouth and his tongue darted in. She felt his erection building. When they came apart she took his hand and placed it over one of her breasts.

"Oh, damn! I never expected anything like this!"

"Are you excited Mr. Todd?" She reached down and felt of his fly, found his long hard lump and smiled at him in the half light. "Yes, you are excited." She opened her blouse and pushed his hand inside. "Play with my titties, Todd. I like it!"

"Jesus!" He kissed her again with his hand on

her breast as she rubbed his crotch. Then she pulled him back into the short alley away from the street and sat down on the ground behind a carriage.

She quickly opened her blouse and lifted the chemise. "Play with them!" she commanded him. Gerry did.

"Show me your big cock, Gerry Todd," she said softly.

"Oh, damn!" he said. He fumbled at his waist and then his penis sprang out, hard and ready.

While he did this she reached quickly into her pocket and took out the knife. She opened the blade, heard the lock snic into place so the blade could not fold back.

When he looked down at his hard penis, she swung the knife. The razor-like blade slit Gerry Todd's throat from side to side, opening both carotid arteries. Then she grabbed his penis and using the knife, sliced it in half.

She had moved away from the spurting blood from his arteries. None of it splashed on her. His hard pumping heart sprayed blood from his throat as Gerry Todd died in less than a minute.

Colette wiped the bloody knife on the man's shirt, unlocked the blade and folded it, then slid it back into her skirt pocket. She stood, brushed the dust and dirt from her dark skirt, walked back to Main Street, turned right and was soon in her hotel room undressing.

Only for a moment did she think of Gerry Todd. Then his face became that of her older brother who had raped her so many times. She smiled thinly, remembering the blood gushing from her brother's neck. Then she frowned. Or was it Gerry Todd? She wasn't sure.

Colette put on her nightgown, made sure the door was locked and lay down on her pillow. She was smiling as she went to sleep less than two minutes after blowing out the lamp.

17

After Spur left the hotel room and his fruitless talk with the two Englishmen, he went down one floor to his own room in the same hostelry. He was twenty feet away when an explosion shattered the door to his room, blasting half of it into the hall and filling the area with thick smoke.

Spur bent low under the smoke and worked his way to the splintered door. The window had blasted out as well and now the wind blowing in quickly cleared the room of smoke. The place was a mess. The bed had been blown apart. Bedding, springs and mattress parts were all over the room. The dresser had tipped over, the porcelain pitcher shattered against the wash basin.

His carpetbag under the bed had been ripped open and slammed to one side wall. Chunks of plaster from half the ceiling had fallen over everything.

Before Spur started his examination, the hotel clerk came charging into the room.

"What the hell?" he asked.

"Bomb," Spur said. "Most likely dynamite. Not sure how they set it off yet. It wasn't thrown through the window because the glass all blew outside. I locked the door when I left. Of course anyone with a pass key could get in here."

"This has never happened before, Mr. . . ."

"McCoy, Spur McCoy. If it hasn't, then you're lucky." He found what he had been looking for a few minutes later. A white candle, the cheap kind you could buy for three cents in a hardware store, had been blasted against the front wall. He picked it up. It had burned about half way down, leaving a three-inch stub. He showed it to the room clerk.

"Here's how they set off the dynamite. Wedge the candle into a solid place and wrap the dynamite fuse around the candle. When the flame burns down to the fuse, it lights it and sets off the bomb. Simple, effective and can let the bomber be up to an hour away from the scene before the bomb goes off.

"I'm sure you'll pay for the damages, Mr. McCoy."

"I'm sure I won't. I may charge the hotel for damage to my equipment and my clothing. Find the bomber, he's the one who should be paying."

Spur gathered up his clothing and everything else he could find that he owned. "I rented a room on the first floor yesterday, I think it was. I'll move down there. As far as you know Spur McCoy has checked out of his room."

"Yes sir, Mr. McCoy."

In the room that Spur had rented for the Englishmen, he settled in, saw that the bomber had also stolen his backup .45 Colt and two boxes of shells. Swell person. Spur decided he better buy a new weapon and headed for the hardware store which had a selection of handguns.

He walked outside into the late afternoon. It was nearly four o'clock. This far north it would not be dark until nearly nine that evening. He turned toward the store and stumbled on a loose plank in the boardwalk. Just as he pitched forward a rifle snarled from across the street and a slug zapped through the air where his chest had been a split second before.

Spur dove to the ground, rolled on the board-walk and fell off it behind a water trough at the near edge of the dirt street. Two more rifle slugs jolted into the heavy boards of the trough, then Spur heard a horse pounding down the alley at a gallop. He came up with his long barreled Colt but the man was too far away. The black horse was ridden by a tall man in a dark shirt and dark pants.

He headed toward the route south out of town. Spur watched him a moment, saw a cowboy just getting off his horse in front of a saloon.

"Can I borrow your horse, cowboy?" Spur shouted as he ran up to him. "That snake just tried to bushwhack me!"

The cowboy nodded. Spur jumped on the mare's back, slid into the saddle and raced after the gunman. He checked but the cowboy did not have a rifle in his saddle boot. Spur tried to remember how many .45 rounds he had for the Colt. Twenty in his gunbelt, but none in his pockets. He hadn't planned on a shootout.

He rode through the alley, charged to the left where he had seen the rider turn. Now there was only a few houses between him and the prairie. He could see the rider ahead, galloping hard, heading straight at the ridge to the west of town.

Spur slowed his horse. There would be no trouble following the bushwhacker. The river flowed in the other direction. There was little timber this close to town. It was mostly rolling land with a few gentle hills, in an open and wide valley. The gunman was at a disadvantage.

At the first tree, Spur looked ahead and found some small groves of trees. They were mostly ponderosa pine and white pine, with little brush or undergrowth. Not a good spot for another ambush.

Spur rode to the left of the area the man in black would have entered the woods if he continued on his same route. He guessed that the man he chased would find a spot and stand and fight. He was not supplied for a long run. His first move would come from a good position. It was Spur's job not to get caught in an ambush where the gunman could be successful.

At the very edge of the pine grove, Spur stopped and listened. He held the muzzle of his mount but heard no sounds of movement, no call from the other animal. He moved ahead cautiously.

A rifle shot blasted in the virgin wilderness, and at once Spur knew his horse was dead. She took the slug in the head and collapsed at once. Spur jumped to one side and came up running.

The one shot told Spur a lot about his opponent. The man was a hired killer who would stop at nothing to get his man. No cowboy would shoot a horse, that was a sacrilege. This killer had no such moral cautions.

Spur slid behind a big pine and looked to the left where he figured the shot had been fired.

There were fifty yards of open space with only scattered trees, then a spate of heavy brush that could conceal the killer and his horse.

Spur began moving toward it from tree to tree. He changed directions so the gunman could not get a bead on him for the next charge.

When he had covered half the distance he stopped and listened again. This time he heard a horse blowing somewhere ahead. It was quickly cut off as if hands had grabbed the muzzle.

Good, the man was still with his horse. Easier that way.

Spur charged to the next tree, a slender foot thick pine that afforded inadequate protection from a rifle, and at once he changed angles and jolted to a two-foot tree at right angles to his main line of attack.

A rifle shot barked into the quietness and the sharp sound was swallowed up by the green foliage. It missed. Spur stopped behind the big tree and worked on his attack plan. Right now he had little to go on. The man might have a whole box of shells, or he could have brought only three or four in his pocket, planning on a quick kill in the street and then fade into the townlife.

His best bet: no six-gun, one rifle, a knife probably and not more than a dozen rifle rounds. He had used three in town, and three more so far. He was down to six rounds. Maybe.

One was enough to kill.

Spur checked his next tree. It was fifteen yards away. Plenty of time for a good marksman to sight in and fire. If Spur ran a yard a second it would give the rifleman fifteen seconds. Too long.

Spur checked other trees. None good enough. He found a good sized rock directly behind his tree. It was hand sized. He threw it the opposite way he was going to run, aiming it at some small brush so it would make some noise.

As soon as the rock hit, Spur darted for his tree. The noise should pull the gunman's attention away from the point where Spur had been last seen.

When Spur was four strides from the tree, the rifle spat out blue smoke and hot lead. But the aim had been hurried. The lead only sliced through Spur's pantleg by his ankle, missing flesh and bone. Then he was safely behind the tree.

Now he was within ten yards of the hiding spot. Spur saw the blue smoke where the shot had been fired. He edged his long barreled Colt around the tree and sent a .45 slug into the brush three feet to the left of the smoke.

"Fire and move, fire and move." His old infantry training was still practical, lifesaving. He counted on most men being right handed and most would roll to the right after firing.

Spur heard no sound of pain from the brush.

He had twenty-four rounds left.

From this point the trees grew closer together. In one strong surge he could top the small rise and see behind the shield of brush. As Spur was getting ready for the move, he heard the sound of saddle leather creaking. The man was riding out!

He surged around the tree and charged the ten yards to the break.

The tall, gaunt man had just settled in the saddle on a big roan. Spur lifted his iron and fired all in one shot. The lead blasted into the left shoulder of the bushwhacker as the mount charged forward. Before Spur could aim another shot the pair plunged into the light brush and were gone.

Spur ran into the spot he last saw the horse only to find it vanishing into another clout of brush thirty yards downslope.

McCoy dropped to the ground on his knees, and pushed two more rounds into his pistol. He would carry six rounds now and take the chance. He had wounded the man, a tall, dark, lean individual Spur couldn't remember seeing before.

The man was hurt. That would slow him down.

The bushwhacker might be a local. If so he wouldn't run, he would try to finish his job or go back to town and get his shoulder treated.

Now Spur had the advantage. He ran toward the brush and as he suspected the killer was not waiting for him, Spur eased through the small growth and looked out into an open area of two hundred yards.

Near the far side he saw the roan standing behind two big ponderosa pines. He could not see the man. Much too far out of range for even Spur's long barreled Colt. But fish-in-a-barrel range for the rifle which Spur figured was a Sharps by the sound.

Spur edged back out of sight so he could watch the area where he figured the gunman had to be. The stranger had taken the first advantage. Kill the victim's horse and put him on foot. He had another advantage with his long gun, but so far that had not been the controlling factor.

Spur ran to the left. He was a natural warrior. He did not sit down and logically figure out his moves. If he had to do that he would be as good as dead in a combat situation. He had learned that in his days in the Civil War as an infantry officer.

Instinctively he knew what to do and how to do it.

The Secret Service Agent slanted around the clearing and past the big ponderosas toward the still visible horse. Almost too late he realized it could be a trap. The horse was visible but not the man.

Trap!

He slowed, bellied down beside a white pine and edged up so he could look around it at ground level. Few men will watch for a an attacker on the ground. He scanned all the area around the twin ponderosas but could find no evidence of a man. He sectionalized the area, concentrating on each square yard of the trees and brush at one time.

In one spot a foot-high pine tree leaned at an unnatural angle as if an elbow or a shoulder nudged it to one side. If it had been trampled with a boot it would be righting itself gradually. He watched, it did not move. Then it did! depressing a little more.

Spur was forty yards away. He leveled out the long-barreled Colt and sighted in. With both hands he held the weapon and refined his sight again just to the right of the small pine.

McCoy fired six rounds into the area as fast as he could pull the trigger. He had practiced holding the weapon solid against the recoil for fast shooting. His sturdy hands and wrists were like steel.

He saw the first bullet slam through the light brush exactly where he wanted it and the other five made a pattern around the spot.

A scream of rage slanted through the silent pine trees.

Quickly Spur kicked out the spent brass and

shoved in six more loads from his gunbelt.

He saw no movement among the brush.

Spur ran again.

This time he took more chances. A rifle round whispered over his head but he was behind a tree again, then he jolted forward, circling the spot where the enemy lay.

The attacker was still alive.

He was still deadly.

The Secret Service Agent came up from behind where he had seen the brush move. The horse was still in place, tied he could see now, some ten yards from the former target.

Spur lifted his six-gun, concentrating on the same spot where he had seen the small pine tree move.

The suddeness of the rifle shot caught him off guard. The bullet from the Sharps smashed into his Colt on the side of the cylinder, jolted it from his hand nearly breaking his trigger finger. His Colt spun twenty feet to his left. He knew that it would never work again, at least not until it had been retooled by a gunsmith.

Spur shook his numb right hand and hunkered down to where he had rolled behind a pine tree.

What the hell could he do now? His ambusher had killed his only weapon.

Except the four-inch sheath knife on his belt. A knife against a rifle?

A fine way to die.

Spur watched ahead. Nothing. The man was a master at waiting, a cautious, patient man who had everything to lose. McCoy threw a rock to his left.

No reaction.

A cautious, smart man.

Spur checked the terrain again. He was on a slight uphill from his target. A gentle breeze blew down the slope. He reached in his pocket, found a wad of "stinkers" the frontier matches pasted together on a waxy base with sulphur tips. He cautiously gathered long strands of dry grass from around him, wrapped them around a rock until he had a heavy ball that would burn and he could still pitch.

He made three of them, watching the spot where he had seen the haze of blue smoke where the rifle had last spoken.

When the third fire ball was ready, he struck a stinker, lighted one ball, let it burn a moment, then lit the second from the first. He threw the first fire ball toward the dry grass near the bushwhacker's hiding spot. Then lit the third ball and threw the last two in the same direction.

As the second fire ball hit, the rifle snarled twice more, but Spur was already behind his protective pine tree.

The bushwhacker could have only three rifle rounds left. Maybe.

Spur watched the fire balls catch the grass on fire. It would not produce a forest fire, but could smoke out the gunman. The grass blazed up and the fire pushed it forward. It was ten feet from the place he figured the gunman was when a figure lifted up.

Spur stood and threw four hand-sized rocks he had gathered. He thought one of them hit the man. He ran after him, feeling safe for a moment since the smoke concealed him. He jogged around the small patch of flames and ashes and saw the man twenty feet ahead. He was down.

The bushwhacker had lost his rifle. He held his

right, bloody shoulder. His left leg had twisted under him and Spur saw a spot of blood on his pants leg.

Spur took out his sheath knife and walked forward slowly.

"I won't kill you unless I have to," Spur said evenly.

The man made no agressive move.

"Do you have a pistol?"

"No."

"Your rifle out of rounds?"

"Yes."

"That leg broken?"

"Damnit, yes!"

Spur walked up to him. "Stay very still or this blade goes six inches into your spine!" Spur checked his pockets and ran his hands down each leg. He had no hideout gun. Spur looked at the shoulder. It was broken and bleeding. The bushwhacker gritted his teeth.

Spur attempted to move the broken leg, but the man screamed.

McCoy sat down opposite the man and lit a thin, crooked cheroot. As he smoked the man watched him.

"What's your name?"

"Digger."

"Came to see you the other day."

"Didn't want to talk."

"Who hired you to kill the Land Office man?"

"Didn't do that."

"I'm betting you did. Do you want to get back to town?"

"Yeah, sure!"

"Who is going to help you?"

Digger stared at Spur for a long moment, then

snorted. "And you won't unless I tell you. Is that it?"

"About the size of it. You could hop all the way back to La Grande, I guess. On one foot it could take you a week. You'll be dead before then."

"Yeah. No sense fooling you. It was the Englishmen, they hired me. Wanted him dead and the records all burned."

"Swear that in front of a judge?"

"Sure, if I don't hang. I'll point the finger at them if I only get ten years in prison. I been there before."

"Deal." Spur moved away, came back with a slab of bark two feet long and three stout green sticks the same length.

"I have to splint that leg or you'll lose it. Compound fracture?"

"I guess."

"You'll probably pass out when I do it. But you have my word, you'll get to the doctor before dark."

That's the way it happened. Doctor George promised to keep Digger out of sight for three or four days, and swore his wife and one nurse not to let on he was there.

Spur smiled. He knew who, now all he had to do was smoke them out . . . and find those duplicate land records.

18

The next morning at breakfast, Spur was laying out his day's work. The records were primary. As soon as he found them he could go after the Englishmen. He was sure now the pair of imports from Britain were phonies. An English aristocrat was unlikely to pay someone to murder. Spur, however, knew that he still needed more proof.

He was almost through a big breakfast when a small boy brought him a note and scampered away. Spur opened the lavender scented paper and read.

"Mr. McCoy. My name is Charlotte Younger. I am the sheriff's wife and I must see you this morning. It is an urgent matter. Could I ask you to meet me two blocks in back of the hotel on the corner? I will be in a closed carriage and will stop beside you. This is terribly important to me. Hope to see you there soon. I will be waiting for an hour."

Spur fininished his coffee, folded the note and put it in his pocket. He had worn working clothes for the city, good trousers, boots, a plain white shirt, string tie and his doeskin brown vest.

Outside he read the note again. It must have something to do with the case. Perhaps the sheriff wanted to tell him something but had no other way to get a message to him. Although the logic of the last reason was thin, Spur smiled. He was always ready to see a lady who went to so much trouble to meet him. The closed carriage especially interested him. He had no fears of being ambushed now, since the man who had tried, and who had bombed his room, was safely tucked away with a broken leg, and his good arm was handcuffed to the bedstead.

Spur walked out of the hotel and down the street. He had decided to meet the lady, and walked briskly. He had a lot to get done today and hoped this small detour would not take too long.

He saw the buggy ahead with a prancing black mare in the traces. McCoy walked up to the near side and saw the leather side door with a small glass window in it swing open.

Inside sat a prim lady whom he guessed was short with long, flowing black hair that fell to her waist. She had dark eyes a small smile on her pretty face and a slender, boyish form. She could be about thirty years old.

"Mr. McCoy?"

"Yes, ma'am."

"Come closer, please."

He moved up to the edge of the door and held it. "How can I help you, ma'am? Is it some message from the sheriff?"

"In an indirect way. Would you please get in this door and drive, I need to talk to you."

"Yes, of course."

He stepped into the rig as she pushed over on the seat. Once inside he took the reins, looked out the open front of the rig and clucked at the beautiful black. She stopped prancing and eagerly stepped out as if anxious to get moving again.

"Yes, ma'am?"

"Mr. McCoy, my name is Charlotte, and I just wanted to thank you for the efficient and masterful way that you handled John Ringo. Everyone in town was scared spitless of him. We knew he was a famous gunshark from Arizona and Texas. You see, I had one husband shot down in a gunfight when he was a deputy sheriff. I don't want to lose another one, and John Ringo would have killed Quincy sooner or later if you hadn't been here."

"No way to know that, ma'am."

"Call me, Charlotte, please."

"Yes, all right."

"Would you drive north along the river? There's something I want to show you."

"Ma . . . Charlotte, I really have a lot of work to get done today."

"This won't take long, and I think you'll appreciate seeing this. It isn't far."

They talked about the big land grab and the land office, and he found her intelligent and understanding. Also pretty in a soft casual way.

They came to a heavy growth of trees along the river and she asked him to turn off into the grove through a narrow lane to a point where a house had once stood before it burned down.

When the horse stopped, she got out and asked him to follow her. They walked five minutes to a spot by the river that was shielded on both sides.

"This is my hideaway when I want to come for a swim," she said. "Would you like a swim?"

"No Charlotte, not just right now."

"Maybe I can persuade you." She caught his neck and pulled his face down to hers and when their mouths met hers was open and she licked his lips until his opened and they kissed long and passionately.

When it ended she had one hand inside his shirt rubbing his chest.

"Spur McCoy, I want to thank you properly the best way a woman can for saving my husband's life. I want to make love to you. And don't deny me the pleasure." She kissed him again before he could move, and then stepped back and unbuttoned her blouse. She wore nothing under it. Before he could react the blouse was off and her small breasts pointed proudly toward him.

"You better hurry and get undressed or I'll be in the water before you will. Don't you see, out here, we don't need any bathing suits!"

She sobered as she unbuttoned the side of her skirt.

"Spur, I don't do this with just anyone. I am determined to thank you for saving my husband's life. After the swim it's your party. Anything, any way you want to."

She dropped her skirt, then one petticoat and was naked. She giggled and ran for the water.

Spur undressed slowly. She was slender with solid hips and small breasts. All that long hair was a delight. He plunged into the water beside her and found the Grande Ronde river only three feet deep. They sat in the cool water, splashed each other and then kissed. He found her breasts under the water and she caught his flaccid penis.

They both laughed and kissed again. Her hair was not wet yet except on the ends.

"Time," he said and they walked out of the cold water to the grass. She was so small he picked her up and put her legs around his waist. Then he adjusted her and bent his knees and gently drove his erection into her wet and throbbing pussy.

"Oh, oh, oh!!!! I've never been had this way. It's wild! Absolutely wild."

Spur pounded into her a minute, then slowly dropped to his knees and forward on his hands, putting her on her back on the grass.

"My ass in the grass!" she said softly and laughed like a teenager.

She kissed him then and pulled away. "Please! Hard and fast, do me hard and fast! I want all of you deep inside me right now!"

He felt his long thick tool strumming her high clit on every stroke and soon she was wailing and screeching like a cat in heat as she climaxed again and again and again.

Her excitement rushed Spur and he exploded before he wanted to, nailing her soft bottom into the grass and shoving it forward with six, eight, then ten powerful strokes.

"Oh, Lord!" she said as the last of the tremors faded from her body. "I'll never be the same. You fuck so hard, so good. I could feel you spurting inside of me! I've never felt that before!"

"Making love outdoors in the grass might just excite you more. You'll have to try it often."

She kissed him and held her arms locked around his neck so he could not come out of her.

"Sweet cock, I'll try it four more times with you right here if you can hold out."

"Why not five or six?"

"It's your party, we'll try for a dozen!"

She unlocked her hands, pushed him away and jumped up.

"Let's play tag in the water!"

They did, for ten minutes. By then her hair was thoroughly wet and she swirled it around her as she swam under water in the clear but cold stream. They both shivered and ran to the grass and lay in the warm sun.

Soon they were kissing and petting and anxious to make love again. This time she was serious and soft and gentle. He played with her small breasts and almost had to seduce her before she let him spread her legs. Then it was so gentle and serious and meaningful that Spur was moved. Just as she climaxed she whispered in his ear.

"Spur McCoy, I . . . I thank you for saving my husband's life."

Afterwards they lay in the sun, feeling its warmth. She told him how her first husband was killed by a wild drunk gunman in a bar in town. She was left with one small son and no income and no means of making a living. She lived with friends for two months, then Quincy Younger a dedicated bachelor of forty-two had married her after a two week courtship. They had two children together.

"Your debt is paid, your thanks given," Spur said.

She rolled over on top of him and pushed one of her small hanging breasts into his mouth.

"Good the debt is paid, now I get one for myself, just for the fucking fun of it!"

She devised the positions, she called the shots, and she wound up chewing on him almost to ejaculation, then moving up and with him on his

back riding him like a stallion until he blasted his
juices halfway through her slender form and she
climaxed at the same time, screeching and
wailing like a wild animal.

A half hour later they dressed each other. Back
at the buggy she took out a towel she had
brought and dried her hair. Then they sat in the
sun until it was totally dry. Soon he drove slowly
back to town.

"Mr. McCoy, if we pass in town, I will not know
you. You see, we've never met. This was a one
time . . . one   time   fuck."   She   giggled,
embarrassed saying the word now with her
clothes on.

"I understand. It was a remarkable gesture by
you, a certain sacrifice, and I am impressed and I
appreciate it. I wouldn't think to impose on you."

She smiled, touched his cheek with her
fingertips. "I must say I am bowled over by you,
Mr. McCoy. If I wasn't married I'd set my cap
and flip my skirt if I had to in order to try to
marry you. You're nice!"

She reached over and kissed his lips gently,
then pushed over to the far side of the buggy seat.

"You better drive me back to town quickly
before I forget my married status and start
crawling all over you . . . again."

They both laughed. Then they talked about the
case he was working on during the twenty minute
drive back. He left the carriage at the edge of
town and walked quickly away. She drove in a
round about way back to her house.

It was almost noon. Spur knew what he had to
do now. Last evening he had found his long
barreled Colt and brought it back to town. He
took it to the best gunsmith in La Grande. All it

needed was a new cylinder and a little bit of align-
ment. The man would have it ready in two hours.
Spur bought a backup Colt .45 to replace the one
stolen and two boxes of .45 rounds. First he
refilled his gunbelt loops, then went back on the
street and walked to his hotel.

He had to find out if the Duke of Wallowa's
man servant was in his room. He asked the room
clerk. The man on duty did not know. Spur went
up to the third floor door and knocked.

For a moment no one answered. Spur knocked
again. He hoped they had not felt the fakery
slipping and run away. After the third knocking,
he heard movement inside.

When Edward Long came to the door it was
plain to see that he was hung over. He could
barely open his eyes. Spur grabbed him by the
shirt front and jerked him into the hall.

"Edward, my man. Just the Englishman I was
looking for. You and I are going for a ride."

19

Spur took Edward Long down the stairs and out the back door of the hotel. In the alley he backed the man against the wooden siding and slapped him twice sharply across the face.

"Mr. Long. You are under arrest. I'm a Federal officer and you and I are going for a walk, and then a ride. If you make any move to disagree or to run, I'll shoot you down without a quiver. Do we understand each other perfectly?"

"Y . . . Yes sir."

"Good. This won't take long. You can ride a horse?"

"Every Englishman can ride, sir."

"Not true. We'll see just how good you are forking a quarter horse."

A half hour later Spur and Long had ridden north then west into the sagebrush covered plateau of Eastern Oregon. They could see twenty miles in one direction to the Wallowa mountains. There was little forage on the land for grazing. A lot of sand and scattered sage, clumps of struggling brush in water courses was all. The timber was all in the mountains and foothills.

"Do you know where you are?" Spur asked Long.

"Hell no. Somewhere outside of La Grande."

"Which direction is it?"

"Damned if I know. What do you want from me?"

"The whole thing, the whole swindle with the phony Royal Land Grant."

"Don't know what yer talking about, mate."

"You sure?"

"Damn sure."

"Fine. Dismount."

"You aim to strand me out here?"

"Get off the horse or get shot in the shoulder. Which would you prefer?"

Edward dismounted.

"Take off your shoes and socks and pants."

"What kind of games you playing?"

"We call it barefooted rattlesnake keep-away."

Spur got off his horse, tied the other mount on a lead to his saddle, and walked over to Edward. "Boots, and pants, now."

"I don't understand."

"Tell me about you and Jeffrey or start stripping."

"Nothing to tell."

During the next five minutes Spur got the man's boots, socks and pants, tied them up and put them on his horse. All the time he was telling Edward about the rattlesnakes in the area.

"Not so big, but damn deadly. They have all sorts of names, but most people just call them diamond back rattlers because of the marks on their backs."

Spur found a branch and began turning over rocks. Under the third one he found a rattler. The forked stick nailed the rattler's head to the ground. Spur picked it up holding the deadly snake directly in back of the head so it could not strike at him.

When he carried it to Edward, the smaller man shivered and backed away.

"Get that damned thing away from me! I hate snakes."

"These guys don't like you either. He's real mad by now. I'll just drop him here near you. Don't worry about him. One strike and you're as dead as a bloated steer."

Spur dropped the snake in front of Edward. It coiled for a moment, rattled the ten buttons on its tail, then uncoiled and slithered away.

Spur mounted and rode a dozen yards off. "You think over my proposition, Edward. You tell me everything I want to know, and just maybe you won't have to dodge rattlesnakes trying to find your way back to La Grande."

"Noooooooooooooooooo! You can't do this to me!"

"Why not? I don't hear any citizen complaining. You're just an alien without funds, and my guess without proper papers. Why should I listen to you?"

Spur rode a half mile off, found a small pine tree on the edge of the foothills and relaxed under its shade.

He could see Edward standing on one foot, then the other. He tried to sit down, then jumped up.

Two hours later, Spur rode back to the man. Edward stared at him with angry eyes.

"Bastard! Bloody, fucking bastard!"

"That's the spirit. Now it looks like you can talk. The deal is this. First you tell me what you know and I let you live. That's the big one. You tell me all I want from you and you get your clothes back one piece at a time. Eventually you'll be dressed and on your horse."

"Bastard!"

"You think everyone in this country is stupid?"

"So far. Up to you. If I talk will you see that I get a light sentence. No more than five years, maybe deportation?"

"We'll see. I will try. Questions, Long. Sir Jeffrey is a phony. Tell me about you two. Who are you and how did you get here?"

Long looked at the arid land, the rocks where snakes could be hiding. Slowly he began to talk.

He told Spur about jumping ship from a British freighter in New York, and how they worked the East coast for a while with con games and some pickpocketing.

"The Land Grant is a fraud, right?"

"Bloody right. Got the idea in Chicago. Had some printing done, found some paper, had a bottle of old British ink. Then did some research in the Chicago library."

"Who is the artist?"

"Jeff. He's good. Could have made a living that way if he'd had a mind to. Too lazy."

"And you're a dip and a seaman?"

"About the size of it. We had to get to Oregon or Washington to make the Land Grant scheme work."

"First your names. I want your real names, and the address of one of the places in New York City where you stayed. I was born in that town and grew up there so don't try to fool me."

Edward gave it all to Spur who wrote it down with a pencil on a pad from his rear pocket.

"The Land Office. Who burned it down?"

"I never had nothing to do with that! I didn't even know. It was Jeff. His idea. He figured if the land ownership was up in the air anyway, we would have an easier time of it. He talked to somebody here in town and arranged it. A damned bloody surprise to me."

"Who did he talk to?"

"Gent named Digger. But he's long gone from La Grande by now."

Spur tossed him his boots. Edward slipped into them.

"Get on your horse. We're going back to town. Don't tell anybody where you've been or what we talked about. Especially don't tell Jeffrey. I have a man watching the stables, and another watching the stage. If either of you tries to get out of town you'll be hauled off to jail. Is that clear?"

"Damned clear, g'uvnor. I've got your word that I can't get more than five years in the jail house?"

"I'll send that recommendation to the court. Just don't tell Jeffrey a thing about this."

"Righto, mate. I'm bloody tired of running anyway."

They got into town before dusk and Spur let Edward off at the edge of town so he could walk back to the hotel.

After a big dinner, Spur went back to the burned out building where the Land Office had been. This time he concentrated on the small stable building which was intact. It was little more than a lean-to with a front and side walls.

The rear of it was open and down wind. There were two stalls for horses and pegs on the wall to hang harnesses and tack. A feed box to one side held oats and some mixed ground grain. Two bales of hay sat unopened near the front.

The left side seemed more open than the right. He probed with his iron bar again across the stalls, around the bales of hay, and then on the far right hand side. There he hit something hard. Under an inch of dirt he found a trap door four feet wide and about that long.

When he lifted it by the ring, he found it was mainly a root cellar with potatoes, and sacks of apples and some root crops all stored there. But near the back were two large wooden boxes. He dragged one out and saw that it was closed with a hasp and held with a nail.

Inside the box he found sets of record books, smaller than the normal, but all wrapped in oiled cloth to protect them from the dampness.

When he opened the first one he found the set of duplicate land records for the county and the Land Office. He stared at the books, then wrapped them up and put them back. He closed the trap door and covered it with dirt, then straw.

Spur found Sheriff Younger still in his office. He knew they should be moving on the Englishmen as soon as possible. He told him about his run-in with Digger.

"Digger is the man who probably killed Jonas King. He tried to bushwhack me. He's in custody over at Doc George's right now."

"Digger? He's harmless," the sheriff said. "Leastwise we always thought so."

"Digger also likes to set fires. He torched the Land Office and the mayor's house. He did the first one for money."

"Who paid him?"

"The Englishmen. It's all a part of their con game to swindle property owners in town."

"Can we prove it?" the sheriff asked.

"Not yet. I need to make up some official looking arrest warrants, can you help me?"

The sheriff said he could. Then he motioned to Spur. "A man down here I think you need to talk to. From what he tells me, our British friends were hard at work on that land swindle you're talking about."

The man at the desk in a separate office was writing on a yellow pad of paper. He looked up and stopped.

"Hirum, I think you've met Spur McCoy."

The banker stood and held out his hand. "Indeed I have. Do you know what's going on here?"

"Some of it, Mr. Follette," Spur said. "What else is happening that I don't know about?"

"Friend of mine said this English Lord offered to sell him back his own property. Said it was an 'insurance' kind of deed. Then if the federal court ruled in Lord Mountbatten's favor, the man would own his land free and clear. If the court ruled that land grant was invalid it was just a few dollars of insurance money the property owner was out. Simple insurance."

"That ties together," Spur said. "I knew it was a fraud somehow, but I couldn't figure out how they were going to make any immediate payoff."

"Twenty or thirty business men in town must have fallen for the scheme by now," Follette said. "At even two hundred dollars each, that could be over six or seven thousand dollars."

"Sheriff, I'd suggest you put a deputy on the livery stable and make sure our Englishmen don't decide to take a quick night ride anywhere."

The sheriff agreed and left to send a man.

The banker nodded. "So this all ties in with the Land Office fire. If folks were a little worried anyway about the accuracy of their land records, they would be more prone to go along with a scheme like this. What the hell can we do now?"

"We keep them in town, and then we get them to start accusing each other of murder, that's what we do, Mr. Follette."

It was well after dark when Spur got back to the hotel. Spur opened the door to his room and struck a match. When the lamp flamed up into a good light and he put the chimney in place he saw a man sitting on the bed with a six-gun aimed directly at Spur's chest.

"Okay, McCoy, you can quit pretending. Where the hell have you hidden my daughter, Margaret Smith?"

"Is this a joke, Smith? Just because you own the triple R, the biggest ranch in the county, is no sign you can run around with a gun accusing people of crimes."

The man jumped off the bed, but was careful to keep the six-gun trained at Spur.

"No damn joke! If you've got her in another room under some fake name, you better tell me."

"Put the gun away, Smith before you get in trouble."

"When you show me where Margaret is hiding, I will."

"That could be quite a while," Spur said, "because I don't know. The last time I saw your daughter was at your house that first day I was

out there when she was trying to be polite and
you were your usual, nasty, stupid, offensive self.
Now get out of my room. I want to get some
sleep.''

"Not until you tell me where Margaret is.''

"Then I hope you don't mind my taking my
gunbelt off and putting it on the dresser.''

"Easy, keep your hands away from the iron.''

Spur unbuckled the belt, turned and put it on
the dresser. At the same time he wheeled and
lashed out with his left foot in a round kick. He
aimed the blow at Smith's gun hand and the
move caught Smith entirely by surprise, smashed
into his gun hand and jolted the weapon from his
fingers. It fell on the bed. Spur brought his foot
down, spun and slammed his right fist into
Smith's jaw before he could dive for the gun.

The rancher fell on the bed on his stomach and
Spur dropped on him with one knee in his back.
McCoy grabbed Smith's hands and tied them
together behind his back with a rawhide strip.

"Let me up, damn you! You touch that girl and
I'll kill you!''

Spur stood and let Smith roll over and fight the
rawhide a moment.

"Now, Mr. Smith, do you want to start over?
Are you reporting to a peace officer that you have
a missing child?''

"What the hell you talking about? I just told
you. Margaret came into town this morning, said
she was going to stay with a friend of hers. I came
in for some supplies and got the mail. She got
some important mail at the post office pickup
window and I wanted to give it to her. But the
woman school friend admitted she hadn't seen
Margaret.''

"So you assumed that I had captured her and that I've been raping her all day and evening."

"Well, no. But she did take a shine to you that day. I saw it, and she started making wild plans."

"Smith I can charge you with assault with a deadly weapon for pointing that six-gun at me, you know that? I can arrest you and throw you in jail right now. Is that what you want?"

"Hell no. I got a ranch to run."

"You also have three small ranches to rebuild."

"Not until somebody shows up with legitimate land records."

"If I let you go, will you act half way civilized? Your daughter is what, twenty-two or twenty-three? She has a right to live her own life. You can't live it for her."

"You sound just like she did. You put those ideas into her head. She's only twenty."

"Twenty? Lots of women have three kids in tow by that age. You should be horsewhipped. You probably chase off every young fellow who comes courting. Behave, or I'll leave you tied up all night."

"Okay, okay. I'll stop bothering you. Maybe she isn't here."

"You make trouble for anyone else in town and I'll bring my charges tomorrow and you'll serve at least six months in the county jail. You remember that!"

"Yeah. Maybe I have been too strict. Maybe."

Spur cut the rawhide from Smith's wrists, took the rounds out of his six-gun and handed it back to him.

"My advice to you, Smith, is to get a room here, have a good night's sleep and in the morning ride back to your ranch and go to work. Let the girl live her own life.''

Wade Smith muttered profanities under his breath as Spur opened the door and pointed him into the hallway.

20

Spur ushered Wade Smith out of his room and closed the door. The man would have to change his mind about his daughter sooner or later or he would lose her completely.

The Secret Service Agent was in the middle of checking and cleaning his newly acquired six-gun when a knock sounded on his door.

Spur opened the panel and began talking before he saw who was there. "Smith I told you that I . . ."

Colette, the saloon singer, stood there with a big smile watching him.

"I'm not Smith, but may I come in anyway? We need to talk."

"It's late."

"I know, I just finished singing at the Sage-brush." She walked in and he closed the door.

"Colette, if it's about the other night."

"It is about that. I don't think . . . no I'm certain that I have never been more thrilled, more delighted, or more happy. I want to marry you!

Will you be my husband?'' She laughed. "I guess I should at least show you what you will be getting.'' She unbuttoned the top of her form fitting dress.

"Colette, I'm not sure this is a good idea. You seemed so hesitant the other time.''

"I was a virgin, you had to seduce me. Now I'm more experienced.'' She opened the top of her dress, then walked up to him. "Kiss me a few times, before you decide,'' she said. She reached up and kissed him. For the second kiss she opened her mouth. Then she sat down on the bed, pulling him with her, stretching out and urging him on top of her.

She looked up at him and smiled. "Yes, I think I like this. It feels good with you on top of me. Play with me. Undress me. Spur McCoy do anything you want to with me!''

Spur moved to one side and sat up.

She sat up beside him.

"Colette, you are a talented lady, a marvelous performer, you are a beautiful woman. Why are you throwing yourself at me?''

"For love. I want love. I want you to make love to me and marry me and keep me safe. I don't want to hurt anyone else!''

"I don't understand. How can you hurt people? You make them happy by singing for them.''

"Yes, but I hurt some, too.'' She lifted up and raised her skirts and quickly took the dress off over her head. She took off her chemise and sat beside him bare breasted. "Play with them, pet my titties!''

Her breasts were large, with sturdy nipples that already had swollen with her excitement. When he touched them she moaned and her

nipples stood out taller. Spur bent and kissed her
mounds, licked her nipples and she leaned down
and kissed his neck.

"That is so wonderful, so good!" Her hands
fumbled at his crotch. "Please show your big one
to me, Spur. Please get him out right now!"

Spur sucked half of one breast into his mouth
and chewed on it, then came away and opened his
fly. A moment later his erection popped out, hard,
pulsating and ready.

"Oh, yes!" Colette whispered. Her right hand
slid into the pocket of the skirt of the dress she
had dropped beside her. Spur saw her hand move
and wondered about it.

"Kiss my titties again! That feels so
wonderful!"

Spur did but watched her right hand. He saw it
come away from her skirt with a folding knife.
She moved it over his back and her other arm
brushed his back as it came up.

The Agent listened and he heard a small snic
when a metal sound came from behind him. He
quickly rolled away to the left and lifted his hand
to grab her right wrist which held the open four-
inch blade that was locked in place.

She tried to stab him. He powered her arm
down so the knife drove into the bedding.

"Noooooooooo," Colette wailed. "I didn't want
to do it. You're the only one who has ever been
kind and gentle with me. The only one. I didn't
want to hurt you!"

She cowered back, dropped the knife and pulled
the dress over her bare breasts. "Don't look at
me!" she commanded.

"Colette, I won't look if you tell me all about it.
Tell me about the first time a man molested you."

Her eyes were open wide and she looked right through him for a moment. Then she nodded. "Yes, I can do that. But first you turn around so I can get dressed." She hesitated. "Unless you are too . . . worked up. My brother used to say that. He would say he was too excited, too worked up to stop."

Spur turned around. "Go on, Colette. Tell me about your brother."

She pulled on the chemise and then let the dress down over her head. When Colette had the buttons up the front all fastened, she told Spur he could turn around. She sat primly in the straight backed chair. Spur sat on the bed.

"My brother Zach was older than me. I must have been about thirteen at the time and we lived on a little farm with a few pigs and two cows and some dogs. My brother was always feeling horny and he tried to touch my breasts whenever he could. We used to watch the dogs mating and laugh and he'd say he wanted to do that. I'd laugh and say all he had to do was catch the old bitch dog and try.

"Then one day the folks were gone to town in the wagon and he came in my room in the house. He said this was the day he was going to fuck my cunt just the way the male dog did the bitch. I knew what he meant but I'd never heard those words before.

"I was well developed at thirteen. My breasts were as big as they are now and he always wanted to play with them. Now he came over to me and stripped me to the waist. He was rubbing his crotch as he just looked at me and then he pushed me down on the bed and began playing with my boobies and kissing them.

"Then he began to moan and sweat. He pulled out his thing and pushed it against my stomach and began pumping his hips and he spurted his juice all over my tummy.

"That didn't stop him, he pulled off my skirt and my drawers and played with me. I told him not to, and I cried and tried to beat on him with my fists. He slapped me and told me to shut up, and then he was hard again and pushed his thing into me.

"It hurt awful and I cried and screamed the whole time. He just laughed and said I was a tease. He fucked me three more times before the folks were due to come home. Then he put his pants on and ran out and began shocking the cut hay the way he was supposed to be doing."

"I never told Ma. I knew she'd tell Pa and he would beat up on my brother Zachary. Pa might have killed him. But then every time after that we were alone Zach wanted to do it. He called it fuck-fuck and he was always ready. When Ma wasn't looking he'd grab my breasts or try to stick his finger in my crotch.

"The next time I let him, thinking it might feel better, but it hurt again and I screamed and we almost got caught."

"He planned to get me alone then, down in the field, by the river, even in the haymow.

"I was afraid I'd get pregnant the way the old bitch dog did, and I told him to stop. I got a stick I carried and I hit him a few times. Then he grabbed the stick and slapped me hard and fucked me four times. I was so sore I didn't want to go to the bathroom.

"That went on for more than a year, maybe a year and a half. He knew when he had time and the right place. He'd catch me every two or three days and pump away. I was too scared to tell anyone.

"I decided that was enough. By then I had put up with it for way too long. I was almost fifteen and had a nice boy I wanted to marry when I turned sixteen. He wanted me too, course I never told him about Zach and what he did.

"I bought this knife in town and made a pocket in every skirt I had and I always carried the blade. The first time I opened it and waved it at Zach and scared him off.

"The last time I forgot it until he had my breasts bare. We were in the cornfield and the tall corn really hid us. When I remembered the knife I grabbed it and opened the blade. He slid down on my legs and spread them ready to enter me.

"I slashed the sharp knife out wildly. It cut across his throat and he looked at me in surprise and then horror. I slashed his stiff cock too, cutting it almost in half, then he fell to the side and I got up and dressed and ran through the corn.

"I never looked at him. But I knew he was cut bad. I'd seen Pa bleed a butchered calf by slitting his throat. I cleaned off my knife and hid it in the barn, then ran in the house and was sick all over the kitchen floor.

"Ma put me to bed. They found Zach two days later and the sheriff said must have been attacked by some runaway slaves, or maybe just a drunken no-good."

She went to the pitcher and had a drink of water.

"Ever since then, Spur, when a man molests me, I try to use my knife on him."

"Have you used it here in La Grande?"

"Yes. Twice I think. I get so confused. Every man becomes Zach and he's leering at me, bending over me, hurting me and I slash out at him and it's somebody else I hurt. I'm really only trying to hurt Zach."

"I understand, Colette. It's a sickness. There are doctors who can help make you well."

"I'd like that. I hate it when I use the knife."

"We could throw it away."

"I'd only buy a new one. I've tried that a dozen times."

"Colette do you know how many men you have hurt thinking they were Zach?"

"One every couple of weeks. I don't know. I'm twenty-four now. It's been a long time since I was fifteen."

Spur's brows raised. Twenty-five a year for nine years!"

"Colette, would you like to rest here for the night? You can have the bed, I'll sit up in the chair."

"No, I'll go back to my room."

"It might be better if you stayed here. I'll keep anyone else from bothering you. Some of the men in town know which room you live in here."

"All right. Let me go get my nightgown and some things."

Spur went with her. When she came back she acted as if she were alone, undressing, putting on her nightgown, then turning out the light without another word to Spur. He stretched out on the floor on a spare blanket and snoozed lightly. Every time the springs squeaked as Colette moved, Spur became wide awake. He had no desire to join the nearly two hundred men Colette must have cut or killed with her folding knife.

In the morning Colette was embarrassed to find herself in his room in her nightgown. She made him go outside while she dressed. She remembered nothing of the time she had spent in his room.

"Did we . . . I mean were we . . . intimate?"

"We just talked. You told me about Zachary, your brother."

She frowned. "Yes, I remember him. He hurt me."

"He also made you ill, Colette. There are doctors who can help you. This morning we'll go over and see Doctor George. He'll know where you can go for treatment."

"Then I won't get to sing anymore?"

"I'm sure you'll be able to sing every evening, just like now, only for a different audience."

They had breakfast in the dining room at the hotel, then walked slowly to Dr. George's. Spur explained the situation privately to the doctor.

"Mentally over the edge," Dr. George said. "There's a state hospital in Salem where they are starting to take in people like Colette. She'll be safe there at least. I don't know how much treatment she will get. But it's the first step."

"She's a talented performer, Doctor George. I don't know if you've heard her sing or not, but she's good. Be sure to tell them that so she can perform for the other patients."

"Yes, that would be good for her. I'll keep her here for a day or two, then have someone go with her to Salem. The county can help with the cost."

"Good. How is Rebecca King?"

"Much better. There will be little scarring on her face and arms. She was a lucky lady."

Spur thanked the doctor and hurried on to the

sheriff's office. He had to get the right papers made out as quickly as he could. There were horses the Englishmen could steal if they were desperate enough to leave. He just hoped that Edward Long had not caved in and confessed his blabbermouthing to Spur.

At the sheriff's office the clerk wrote out the warrants of arrest. They made out one for Phineas J. Bull, alias Jeffrey Mountbatten. The charge was grand larceny, conspiracy, and murder of Jonas King.

A second warrant was written for Edward Long, charging him with conspiracy, grand larceny, fraud and pickpocketing.

A third warrant, all carefully written by hand by the clerk, charged Phineas J. Bull with armed robbery in New York City, and listed his New York address.

The last warrant was for Digger, also known as Alan Underwood, for the murder of Jonas King, and arson of the Land Office house and the Mayor's residence.

Spur told the sheriff about Colette.

"We have two recent murders, both with a knife. The first one could have come out of Colette's window. We'll mark them solved. Too damn bad."

Spur told the sheriff that the missing land records had been found.

"Great!" Sheriff Younger said. "That takes one hell of a lot of worry out of this. With the land records back in place, we'll have no more problems with the big ranchers. Wade Smith will be forced to rebuild and restock those three ranches. And the whole problem of the Royal Land Grant will be labeled a hoax."

"Let's go get those records and store them in the bank vault until the county can build a new county clerk's office," Spur said.

The sheriff went with Spur and two deputies, and the men carried the two wooden boxes into the back door of the bank where the boxes were opened. Hirum Follette agreed to store the records and to keep them safe.

"Those books are worth more than their weight in gold," Hirum said. "We'll take good care of them."

21

Spur and Sheriff Younger talked with Hirum Follette, the banker for a few more minutes, then Hirum went over to the hotel to find the Englishmen. There were two ranchers waiting in the hall in front of Hirum just outside Sir Jeffrey's door. He knew both of them.

"Will, this guy is a fraud," Hirum told one of the men. "There is no way legally that he can sell you what you already own. It's a confidence game, a fraud. I can guarantee that the land records are safe and that they will be found. Don't tell anyone."

Will watched the banker. He had known Hirum for ten years. Slowly he nodded. "If you say so, Hirum. But if that is so, why are you here?"

"Working with the sheriff, Will. We're about ready to trap these Englishers and arrest them."

Will smiled. "You dang double sure about the land records?"

"Positive, Will."

The man leaning against the wall shook

Hirum's hand. "If you say our land is safe, I'll go along with you, Hirum." He whispered to the man next to him and they both walked along the hall and went down the stairs.

A minute later the door opened and a man Hirum knew only casually came out. Edward Long peered out after the man left.

"I guess you're next, sir," he said. "Right this way."

Hirum walked into the room and saw Sir Jeffrey busy at a small desk.

"Good morning, my good man. And what can we do for you today?"

"A friend of mine said you had a kind of insurance policy I could buy on my bank and three stores I own, is that right?"

"It certainly is. My name is Jeffrey Mount-batten," he said holding out his hand.

Hirum took it and shook. "Hirum Follette. Be interested in what kind of a deal you have."

"Straightforward and simple, Mr. Follette. I give you a legal and binding bill of sale and grant deed for your property. As you must have heard from your friend, if the disputed Royal Land Grant I have is valid, I own this land. But with this insurance I have already sold your former property back to you at a low, low, bargain price. In the event the Land Grant is declared not valid, you still own your land, and you are out only the 'insurance' fee we charge."

"Sounds reasonable. How much is the fee?"

"For your four parcels, we could give you a bargain price, Mr. Follette. Usually we charge four hundred dollars a property, regardless of size or location. But since you have four of them, we could accommodate you for two hundred and fifty dollars each, or a total of a thousand dollars. That's a six hundred-dollar discount!"

"Sounds reasonable. I understand you deal only in cash?"

"Yes, that's right."

"All right, draw up the papers and I'll sign. Then I'll get the cash for you from my assistant who is outside. As you see, Sir Jeffrey, I am a banker, a cautious man."

Jeffrey Mountbatten smiled. "I can see that, Mr. Follette, and the people of Wallowa county are lucky to have a man of your intelligence and caution safeguarding their life savings." He worked for a moment on some papers on the desk.

"Now if you would give me the names of these properties."

Hirum did and Jeffrey worked again on the papers.

"All right, we're ready. You inspect them, and sign them. Then as soon as I get the money, I'll sign and the deal will be complete.

Five minutes later the details were finished. A clerk from the bank waiting in the hall gave Hirum a valise with two thousand dollars in it. He counted out the thousand and Jeffrey signed the documents. The clerk took the valise and went out the door.

That was the signal. Spur McCoy, the sheriff and two deputies burst into the room and arrested Jeffrey.

"I don't understand," the Englishman said.

"You, Phineas J. Bull, alias Jeffrey Mountbatten, formerly of 1476 Fourteenth Street in New York City, are under arrest for fraud, conspiracy, and the murder of Jonas King."

"No! there must be some mistake!

"Are you Phineas J. Bull?"

"Never heard of him."

"We have a witness who will swear that is your real name. Also that you are not a real Lord, that you are a merchant seaman who jumped ship in New York."

One of the deputies took the thousand dollars in greenbacks off the desk.

"This money is evidence for your trial, Bull," the sheriff said.

Spur looked in the far room. No one was there. He checked the third room in the suite and found it too was empty. Then Spur found the second outside door that led into the hall. He looked out the window and saw a man rush out of the hotel on the street below, grab a horse that had been tied to the rail and jump aboard.

The man was Edward Long.

Spur raced down the three flights of steps to the street, borrowed a horse from a stranger and gave chase. That reminded him he had to pay for the horse Digger had shot. He caught up with Long half a mile out of town and put two pistol rounds over his head. Long brought the horse to a stop and lifted his hands.

"Going somewhere, Long?" Spur asked as he rode up.

"Thought it might be a bloody good idea. You had us cold and hard with no place to fudge."

"About the size of it. Our deal is still good if you can prove you didn't help in planning the killing."

"Bloody right bout that, mate. Surprised the hell out of me, it did."

Spur took the valise off the Long's saddle horn.

Inside were packets of greenbacks. Spur guessed the total at eight or nine thousand dollars.

"You took your spending money with you, I see," Spur said. "A lot of merchants in town are going to be unhappy with you two."

"His doing, I'm just his lowly man servant."

"That's your role in this stop. I'd wager at the next town you are Sir Edward Long, Duke of Kent or some such, and Jeffrey is your man servant. You probably take turns."

"How in the bloody hell did you know that?"

Back in town, Jeffrey Mountbatten, or more correctly Phineas J. Bull, was in jail. Edward joined him in a separate cell. Spur had explained to the sheriff the deal he had made with Long. It should hold up.

Two deputies brought Digger over to join the jail bird crew.

The sheriff had set up a table inside the office and was checking records that Bull had kept, and paid back the money the merchants had spent so unwisely for insurance.

The sheriff kept the thousand dollars from the banker for evidence.

Sheriff Younger knew that paying back this fake insurance money should cement his re-election for three or four more terms.

The sheriff sent a letter to the Federal court in Portland explaining the arrests and certified that he had a witness who swore that the Royal Land Grant was a hoax, a forgery, and that the court should disregard it.

The county attorney had formally charged the three men with a variety of crimes, and set a hearing for two days hence.

Spur searched out the cowboy in the saloon he

had been headed for, and paid for the man's horse and saddle.

Then Spur relaxed in the sun outside of the sheriff's office for a minute. Already the word was all over town about the swindle, the fakery of the English "Lord" and his part in the death of Jonas King. The word had spread as well that the land records were intact and safe in the bank vault.

Spur felt that the whole community seem to let out a held in breath. To threaten to disenfranchise three thousand people of their property and life's savings had been a terrible strain. The danger was over, they were safe again.

Spur walked down to Doctor George's office and talked to Rebecca King.

"So it's all clear now, Mrs. King. The Englishman hired Digger to burn down the Land Office. Somehow in the process your husband surprised him or the Englishman, we're not sure which, yet, and they killed him so he couldn't talk. He was a fine man, and defended the county property with his life. He will get a medal and a plaque to his honor mounted in the court house. I've arranged it with the sheriff."

Rebecca sat up now and smiled. Her face had healed more and the doctor had been right, there would be almost no scarring.

"I'm glad you were here, Mr. McCoy. Without you it might have remained a mystery, and my husband's killers gone unpunished. I thank you again."

"Oh, by the way. The county is going to need a temporary clerk, until the election at least. The county officials have named you to that post as soon as you are able. I hope that you will run for the office when the election comes."

Rebecca King blinked back tears. Spur patted her hand and left the room.

His next call was on Colette. She would be leaving on the noon stage for Portland.

She wore a different dress now, a simple calico print that swept the floor and buttoned high on her throat and each wrist.

"I'm going on a trip today!" she said excitedly. Her eyes sparkled. "Doctor George says his wife needs to go to Portland, and she's going with me. Isn't that wonderful?"

"I'm glad for you, Colette. I'm sure you'll find some extremely good people in Portland."

She came toward him. "Mr. McCoy, Spur. I know that you helped me. I'm not exactly sure how, I can't remember much of that time, but I thank you." She reached up and kissed his cheek. "Thank you for everything."

Spur patted her shoulder and walked out of the room. He heard the door lock solidly behind him. He hoped that wherever she went they would have a piano she could use.

Back on the street, Spur paused for a moment. He had nothing to do! What a marvelous feeling. All the loose ends had been tied up. He could lay over until the next day and take the stage back to Portland where he could telegraph his office and headquarters.

He decided to change clothes, then have a leisurely lunch and sit in a tilted back chair on the boardwalk in front of the general store for an hour or two to soak up the atmosphere of La Grande. He might not be back this way for some time.

As soon as he walked into his hotel room he knew he was not alone. He closed the door and found Margaret Smith smiling at him.

"Hi cowboy," she said.

"Did your father find you?"

"Not yet. He went back to the ranch this morning, just the way you suggested."

"He'll try to kill me if he finds you here."

"Probably."

She moved forward and put her arms around his neck, then kissed him hungrily. The kiss grew into half a dozen and they soon were sitting on the bed.

"This time my father will think he knows where I am. My woman friend and I are on a horseback ride along the river hunting cattails." She put his hand over her breast.

He hesitated.

"Oh, no! You're rejecting me?"

Spur kissed her to put a lie to the words. "Just thinking about protection. Your father knows about this room. I'm going to go down and rent another one, on the top floor. You wait here."

Ten minutes later Spur and Maggie Smith sat on the bed in the third floor room.

"Why don't you stay over a couple of more days," Maggie said as Spur unbuttoned her dress. "I'm sure we could figure out a few new ways to make love."

"A couple of days? Sounds reasonable. My work here is done, I do need some rest and relaxation."

She unbuttoned his fly and pushed her hand inside the cloth.

"My, my! I certainly know part of you that is not what I'd call relaxed! And I like him that way!"

Spur growled at her and bent her back on the

soft bed. "Maggie, I'm going to show you about a dozen ways that you will like. I hope you have that many new and exciting ideas for me."

"Shut up, McCoy. Get my dress off and show me number one before I explode!"

IF YOU ENJOYED THE ADVENTURES OF SPUR McCOY, BE SURE TO ORDER LEISURE'S RED-HOT *BUCKSKIN* SERIES

2066-1	BUCKSKIN #1: RIFLE RIVER	$2.75 US, $2.95 Can.
2088-2	BUCKSKIN #2: GUNSTOCK	$2.75 US, $2.95 Can.
2126-9	BUCKSKIN #3: PISTOLTOWN	$2.75 US, $2.95 Can.
2168-4	BUCKSKIN #4: COLT CREEK	$2.75 US, $2.95 Can.
2189-7	BUCKSKIN #5: GUNSIGHT GAP	$2.75 US, $2.95 Can.
2229-X	BUCKSKIN #6: TRIGGER SPRING	$2.50 US, $2.95 Can.
2254-4	BUCKSKIN #7: CARTRIDGE COAST	$2.50 US, $2.95 Can.
2271-0	BUCKSKIN #8: HANGFIRE HILL	$2.50 US, $2.95 Can.